Praise for *Switching to Analog*

"A transmission of pure creativity layered with spiritual teachings, a fun read with many layers and activations!"

— Phoebe Conant, *Microdosing Coach*

Switching to

[An•a•log]

KATIE MOSELEY

ISBN: 979-8-9888541-0-4 (Paperback)
ISBN: 979-8-9888541-1-1 (Digital)

Library of Congress Control Number: 5122308567112239

Front cover image by Pulp Studio.
Interior design by Laura Jones-Rivera.

Printed in the United States of America.

Denver, Colorado

www.electrickatieland.com

"Beyond the restless flowing electricity of life is the ultimate reality—
The Void. Your own awareness, not formed into anything possessing
form or color, is naturally void. The Final Reality. The All Good.
The All Peaceful. The Light. The Radiance. The movement is the
fire of life from which we all come. Join it. It is part of you."
-Timothy Leary

DEDICATION

This book is dedicated to all the Starseeds who volunteered to come to Earth. Infinite love and blessings to all on this journey. May you find the path through the amnesia and re-member with love. To my daughters, who are of a galactic nature—thank you for helping me stay the course and tap into the toroidal field of the heart space. I see the stars in your eyes.

144

Data Entry
Time: 9:08 PM MST
17 July, 2020
Dose: 2 hits of Love

[Star Hawk] Howdy! Star Hawk, here…

[Electric KT] Logging on…

[Star Hawk] Do you copy? I dropped some acid this afternoon.

[Electric KT] Copy that. You were fading, but just came back into frequency. What level are you working with?

Reports confusion. His programming is being unveiled. He is distracted by the colors. They comfort him as everything surfaces. He's in a frequency bubble, just barely matching into mine through the waves.

[Electric KT] Just know that whatever you see and think when you're tripping—it's all real. It's a hologram and your mind creates the universe for your soul.

Climb enough rocks and you'll figure it out.

The light will shine down upon you, and you'll be like, "oh damn, I get it now!" And then you'll realize you could have been fucking that hot spiritual lady with the heart of gold this whole time. It's true. My heart is a rainbow of pure love mixed with insatiable sexual desires for silly boys on acid.

Okay, I'm glad we had this talk.

< Send >

[Star Hawk] Preeeeeeety neat!

He's dazzled.

[Electric KT] I want to meet you where the ropes are made of stars.

[Star Hawk] Someday sweetheart. Someday.

Data Entry
Time: 8:57 PM MST
8 August, 2020
Sun Sign: Leo

Tele-pathy
tuh·leh·puh·thee

"Communication between minds by some means other than sensory perception."

[Electric KT] ⚠ I know you. ⚠ [Star Hawk]

I was waiting for you.

Come be with me.

NOW.

[Electric KT]

Translation:
"pure shining light"

Origin: 11D
Time: 9:55 PM MST
Space-Time: Coordinates Unknown
Mission: Assist 3D to 5D Transition
Earth Age: approximation 41 Years
Soul Age: 44,000 Photons of Light
Soul Pod: Healers, Seers, Guardians
Soul: Starseed

⚠
[Star Hawk]

Translation:
"wanderer"

[Find me again.]

4

Data Entry
Time: 2:57 PM MST
9 August, 2020
Sun Sign: Leo

[Star Hawk] I love it when you suck my cock.

◆Moves climbing gear◆

[Electric KT] You make me so {WET::WET}{WET::WET}{WET::WET}
{WET::WET}{WET::WET}{WET::WET}{WET::WET}{WET::WET}{WET::WET}
{WET::WET}{WET::WET}{WET::WET}{WET::WET}{WET::WET}{WET::WET}
{WET::WET}{WET::WET}{WET::WET}{WET::WET}{WET::WET}{WET::WET}
{WET::WET}{WET::WET}{WET::WET}

✧ ⚠::\\ [Electric KT] ::\\Merge//:: [Star Hawk] //::⚠ ✧

Yes

Yes

Yes

Yes

Yes

Yes

Yes

Yes

Yes

Yes

Yes

Yes

Yes

{STARS::STARS} ✧ {STARS::STARS} ✧ {STARS::STARS} ✧
{STARS::STARS} ✧ ✧ ✧ ✧ {STARS::STARS} ✧ {STARS::STARS} ✧
{STARS::STARS} ✧ {STARS::STARS} ✧ {STARS::STARS} ✧ ✧ ✧ ✧ ✧ ✧ ✧
✧ ✧ ✧ ✧ ✧ ✧ ✧ ✧ ✧ ✧ ✧ ✧ ✧ ✧ ✧ ✧ ✧ ✧
✧   ✧ ✧ ✧ ✧ ✧ ✧ ✧ ✧ ✧ ✧   ✧
✧   ✧ ✧ ✧   ✧

Data Entry
13 August, 2020
Time: 4:39 PM MST
Dose: Changa Dreams

[Electric KT] I'm going in…

[Transmission]

If you were infinite, wouldn't you want to create a complex experience to explore?
There would be nothing but time, because there is no time.

[Download]

Dimensions are fluid.
Change in a snap with the mind.
We are so powerful.
Love is the original Creation.
Transcending our exploration of lower frequencies.
In one dimension, there was a program implanted to block our connection to love.
It is shown to me like a computer virus, introduced by AI.
It is one of hatred.
It causes us to forget our ability to connect to love.
They use it so they can feed off the lower frequencies.
Some of the programs are introduced at birth, when we moved away from healthy human births and nurturing. The crib is a cage. Immediate programming. Minimal touch. Scheduled.
They took away knowledge of the esoteric. The tools of indigenous and eastern spirituality that allow us to create and connect with love and the other dimensions were removed.
These are the tools to our power as Creators on Earth.
Great Awakening.
We are releasing all low frequency programs.
Undo the filters and programs so we can step into our creation space.

[Vision]

They keep showing me dropping down into the human experience. A Simulation Program.
I was to fully immerse, fully forget, to have all my human experiences, so I can fully understand the programs I am here to help <DEFRAG>.

[Insight]
Help the New Earth. Stop creating from a place of fear and start creating from a place of love. Isn't that beautiful? Thank you for showing me what I already know.

This is the purpose of the New Earth..creating from a place of love...that was the original intention of Earth. Create with the open-hearted innocence of a child. This is love. There is no judgement. The world is full of love—see that and that is the paradigm you will live in and continue to expand.

I don't need to understand all the layers and dimensions.
They showed me how complex it is.
All I need to know is how to anchor in love, teach people how to heal, and how to step into their Creator space.

Anything I think, I create.
Anything I feel, is already done.
Align with it, and it manifests into your stream.

So much love.
All is well.
All transcends.
All is infinite.
No need for attachment to old energy.
Connect with love, gratitude, playfulness, and curiosity every day.

There are no rules. All is malleable.

Able to let go of hurt energy from childhood once the pattern can be seen. The current societal programs trivialize the hearts and innocence of children.
The virus insertion was love = rejection.

Entanglement.
Untangled.
Dense energy lifted.
Full creation space.
Love. All is love.
Let go.
Create.
It feels blissful to be free.
No more darkness.
Light. Light. Light.
Alchemy.
Magick.

Data Entry
Time: 1:01 AM MST
17 August, 2020
Dose: Galactic Frequencies

✧
✧
✧
✧
✧
✧
✧

✧ ✧ ✧ ✧ ✧ ✧ ✧ ✧ ✧ # Starseed ✧ ✧ ✧ ✧ ✧ ✧ ✧ ✧ ✧

✧
✧
✧
✧
✧
✧
✧

[Translation]

"A Crystal in Sentient Life"

A highly advanced spiritual BEing or Soul originating from a distant
planet, solar system, or galaxy.

They embody activation encryptions and special codes designed to unlock
their knowledge, wisdom, and abilities at a predetermined or spontaneous
time.

They are "seeded" into specific civilizations, predominantly those with darker sides, to pave new pathways for innovation, healing, creativity, understanding, expansion, and ascension.

Time travelers from the perceived wave of time. In Truth, they are from another dimension of the quantum field. Vibrating at the Sixth Dimension (6D) or higher when launched.

✦

✦

✦

Strengths: Empathetic, Sense of Purpose, Freedom Seeker, High Earth IQ, Intuitive, Clairvoyant, Spiritually Awake, Emotional, Ancient Wisdom, Energetically Gifted, Curious, Unconditionally Loving.

✦

Likes: Touch, Words, Daydreaming, Astrology, Love, Art, Music, Travel, Magick, Freedom. Sex.

✦

Dislikes: Inauthenticity, Control, Confinement, Violence, Excessive External Stimuli, Limitation, Lies, Darkness.

✦

Weaknesses: Loneliness

✦

Loves: All that is ONE

✦

✦

✦

Data Entry
Time: 7:55 AM MST
27 August, 2020
Dose: 1G Taj Mahal

[Electric KT] Logging on…

The amnesia is thick here on Earth.

Empty Avatars everywhere.

I call them, "The Marionette People."

Find the ones who are…

A

W

A

K

E

[Higher Self] Karate chop your way through this like a ninja from the stars, Electric KT.

Data Entry
Time: 11:26 AM MST
14 September April, 2020
Dose: 1 G Golden Teachers

[Electric KT] Logging on…

Transcending all history. Letting it go. I am a soul of pure consciousness dropping down into the human experience. It is an experience of forgetting my origin completely. To experience it, I must believe it, to be fully immersed in it. The ultimate challenge is to get yourself to wake up out of the dream of this existence. Return to the knowing that you are the creator of the experience.

Ego may want to receive this in another way.

To transcend the body is to accept the death of it as organic matter. Accept that your soul/consciousness exists beyond your body. It is the ultimate lesson in surrendering and the reward is to regain the body. That is the ultimate challenge. You may resist it, but you are on a spiritual journey, which simply means you are a spirit journeying in the human body. This miraculous path is similar to Jesus, Buddha, and all the Ascended Masters. It is a game of physics and consciousness. No religion. No faith. A knowing and understanding of your true essence, that the soul creates the math, creates the science, creates all of it. All is One.

From birth, human consciousness is layered with beliefs, programs, attachments, emotions, & traumas. Transcending those is the way back to the soul. Advanced souls come here for bigger lessons for bigger journeys. The ultimate healing, to transcend the body is letting go of all those beliefs, remembering you are consciousness which literally creates and heals all things. Vibrational electrical frequency healing will become normalized and help transcend the old model of treating the human body. They will learn to heal it with more sophisticated measures that are closely aligned with how our existence in the human experience actually manifests. I am not from here. I have been wondering why people were doing things in these archaic ways. No one else seems to notice, but I am abhorred. I am here as a teacher and a student. Maybe you are too.

Data Entry
Time:6:14 PM MST
25 September, 2020
Dose: Ancient Wisdom

[Electric KT] Logging on…

[Research]

[ETHER]

"Ether is the fifth element, the spirit, or the soul for the spiritual force that air, fire, earth, and water descend from. Ether is the personification of the upper air, God's breath." < Aristotle >

"Ether occupies the space between all objects. Some have experienced it as a bridge between earth and body and heaven and spirit. We know this because when we enter a sacred space, or view a sacred work, we sense the ether is overflowing." < Einstein >

[Definition]

chemistry: a pleasant-smelling colorless volatile liquid that is highly flammable.

literary: the clear sky; the upper regions of air beyond the clouds

</#%_truth_detection_%#\>

{ {{   {{{ BEYOND THE CLOUDS }}}   }} }

Data Entry
Time: 2:43 PM MST
5 October, 2020
Dose: Changa Dreams

Electric KT] I'm going in…

The spiraling checker board appears. They let me past the portal.

[JESTER GUIDES]
Remember, this is all a game.
You will forget the game when you are in the thick of a lesson.
That is how the game works.
You will reach out to other healers to help you sort out the lesson, and this
will help you pull yourself up to the higher frequency and remember.
This is how you expand.
Then you can continue to do your work.
Help others.

[Reflection]
If a healer, who has learned so much, can still get sucked into the illusion,
in the midst of a lesson, imagine how much help others need to navigate
this system.

[Teaching]
I was reminded that others make soul agreements to help us learn lessons.
There does not have to be guilt around this when we make mistakes.
It gets easier as we progress through the lessons quicker.
We don't create as much of a mess in the learning.

[Vision]
I see my future self placing blacked out square window panes over the
entrances to certain timelines.

[Future Self]
I placed these blocks because I knew as my knowledge and psychic skills
grew, I would become curious and want more answers. But to know all the
answers would interfere with my lessons. So I placed the blocks for myself,

so I would not inhibit my own growth.

[Vision]
I am in a place of complete disorientation of space and time. I do not know up from down. I am in multiple planes. Blurry. A vision of me being on my phone. Dejavú. Where am I, if I am watching me crawl to my phone? No. Don't do that. Don't text anyone. Stay away from the cell phone matrix. I pop out of that reality, and into the present dream.

[JESTER GUIDES]
Do you see how disorienting it is? How confusing and believable it is to be trapped inside the game...the illusion? You always ask us the same thing. To show you how it works. You always forget. Do you see now? We made it stronger this time. Can you remember?

[Electric KT]
Did I use my phone? What was that?

[JESTER GUIDES]
A training field. That plane has been discarded now. You are assimilated.

[Reflection]
I always cry on these journeys. In a state of gratitude and deep love for this existence. For the bravery and beauty of all who have chosen to participate. For all trying to find their way out...back to themselves.

THE ULTIMATE QUEST.

The ultimate challenge.
The ultimate reward.
To come out of it, with a deeper sense of love and spectrum of emotions.
Evolved Beings come out of the Earth experience.
It is a part of my evolution.
Teaching is dharma.

Data Entry
Time: 9:02 AM MST
9 October, 2020
Dose: Pure Love

[Electric KT] Logging on…

[Star Hawk] Heyy you on here to be a spiritual mama to guys like me?

[Electric KT] Is that what you need?

[Star Hawk] That's what I want..

[Electric KT] You're adorable:)

[Star Hawk] Climbed this today.. *shares mountain project link*

[Electric KT] Looks like a fun one!

[Star Hawk] It was a little dicey in spots. My partner is tight though. Except for her dog. Fucking dogs everywhere these days.

[Electric KT] You don't like dogs?

[Star Hawk] I'm a nice guy. I'm just not a pet person.

[Electric KT] Awe, why not?

[Star Hawk] I dunno. Don't they kind of shit everywhere?

[Electric KT] Don't humans?

[Star Hawk] Lol. Maybe it's because my sister's cat puked on my shoulder one time when I was a kid. It was disgusting. The smell. Mushy. It was traumatizing.

[Electric KT] Oh yeah, that one would be hard to swipe from the memory file.

[Star Hawk] I'm taking a walk up to Table. Crap. There's another damn dog! They're everywhere.

[Electric KT] Dog planet.

[Star Hawk] Prison Planet, with feces.

[Electric KT] I know, I know. That's why they need all the soft and fluffies. How else are they gonna survive this place?

[Star Hawk] Aren't plants and rocks enough?

[Electric KT] Awe, don't you like my cat?

[Star Hawk] Okayy…actually your cat's pretty cool. I like how she's kinda cross-eyed. Silly kitty.

[Electric KT] There he is..Star Hawk's soft and fluffy side. I like it:)

[Star Hawk] You're a sweet gal:) I want to be on that rock all day. You feel me? I like those fat cracks. That's where I crush it. Feels so free.

[Electric KT] Freedom is sooo good. We seeded all these plants for free. The Earth is sooo beautiful. It makes me sad they poison everything.

[Star Hawk] All the GMOs. They're fucking it up.

[Electric KT] I know.

[Star Hawk] They straight up put formaldehyde in the bread. Zombie people.

[Electric KT] I know. Zombie bread:(

[Star Hawk] The seeds *were* free, but they charge people quadruple for the fruit! Unless they're the poisoned ones. No nutrients.

[Electric KT] It's wrong.

[Star Hawk] Nothing but a bunch of plant charlatans down here.

[Electric KT] For real.

Data Entry
Time: 10:32 AM MST
12 October, 2020
Dose: of childhood

[Electric KT] Logging on…

[POISONING LOG]

While on Earth I was forced to eat:

7:30 AM CST
<Insert:Ingredients> WHOLE GRAIN CORN, SUGAR, RICE FLOUR, CORN SYRUP, CANOLA OIL, SALT, TRISODIUM PHOSPHATE, NATURAL AND ARTIFICIAL FLAVOR, RED 40, YELLOW 6, BLUE 1 AND OTHER COLOR ADDED, CITRIC ACID, MALIC ACID.

<Insert:Ingredients> FILTERED WATER, CRANBERRY JUICE (WATER, CRANBERRY JUICE CONCENTRATE), APPLE JUICE (WATER, APPLE JUICE CONCENTRATE), NATURAL FLAVOR, MALIC ACID, PECTIN, FUMARIC ACID, SODIUM CITRATE, ASCORBIC ACID (VITAMIN C), SUCRALOSE, RED 40, ACESULFAME POTASSIUM.

11:30 AM CST
<Insert:Ingredients> CITRIC ACID, POTASSIUM CITRATE, SODIUM CITRATE, ASPARTAME (PHENYLKETONURICS: CONTAINS PHENYLALANINE), MAGNESIUM OXIDE, MALTODEXTRIN, CONTAINS LESS THAN 2% OF NATURAL FLAVOR, ACESULFAME POTASSIUM, SOY LECITHIN, YELLOW 5, ARTIFICIAL COLOR.

<Insert:Ingredients> ROASTED PEANUTS, SUGAR, HYDROGENATED VEGETABLE OIL (COTTONSEED, SOYBEAN AND RAPESEED OIL) TO PREVENT SEPARATION, SALT.

<Insert:Ingredients> CONCORD GRAPES, CORN SYRUP, HIGH FRUCTOSE CORN SYRUP, SUGAR, FRUIT PECTIN, CITRIC ACID, SODIUM CITRATE.

3:30 PM CST

<Insert:Ingredients> UNBLEACHED ENRICHED FLOUR (WHEAT FLOUR, NIACIN, REDUCED IRON, THIAMINE MONONITRATE {VITAMIN B1}, RIBOFLAVIN {VITAMIN B2}, FOLIC ACID) , CANOLA OIL , PALM OIL , SUGAR , SALT , LEAVENING (CALCIUM PHOSPHATE, BAKING SODA) , HIGH FRUCTOSE CORN SYRUP , SOY LECITHIN , NATURAL FLAVOR.

<Insert:Ingredients> WHEY, CANOLA OIL, MILK PROTEIN CONCEN-TRATE, CHEDDAR CHEESE (MILK, SALT, CHEESE CULTURE, ENZYMES), CONTAINS LESS THAN 2% OF MILK, SALT, SODIUM CITRATE, SODIUM PHOSPHATE, CALCIUM PHOSPHATE, LACTIC ACID, AUTOLYZED YEAST EXTRACT, SODIUM ALGINATE, SORBIC ACID AS A PRESER-VATIVE, MILKFAT, CHEESE CULTURE, ENZYMES, NATURAL FLAVOR, COLOR (APOCAROTENAL, ANNATTO EXTRACT).

<Insert:Ingredients> SUGAR, FRUCTOSE, CITRIC ACID, CONTAINS LESS THAN 2% OF ASCORBIC ACID (VITAMIN C), ARTIFICIAL FLAVOR, CALCIUM PHOSPHATE, ARTIFICIAL COLOR, RED 40, BHT (PRE-SERVES FRESHNESS).

5:30 PM CST

<Insert:Ingredients> TOMATOES (WATER, TOMATO PASTE), ENRICHED FLOUR (WHEAT FLOUR, MALTED BARLEY FLOUR, NIACIN, REDUCED IRON, THIAMINE MONONITRATE, RIBOFLAVIN, FOLIC ACID), LOW MOISTURE PART SKIM MOZZARELLA CHEESE (PART SKIM MILK, CHEESE CULTURES, SALT, ENZYMES), PEPPERONI MADE WITH PORK, CHICKEN AND BEEF (PORK, MECHANICALLY SEPA-RATED CHICKEN, BEEF, SALT, CONTAINS 2% OR LESS OF: WATER, DEXTROSE, SPICES, SMOKE FLAVORING, LACTIC ACID STARTER CULTURE, SODIUM ASCORBATE, FLAVORING, GARLIC POWDER, SODIUM NITRITE, BHA, BHT, CITRIC ACID, CONTAINS ONE OR MORE OF: PAPRIKA, OLEORESIN OF PAPRIKA), WATER, CONTAINS 2% OR LESS OF: YEAST, PALM OIL, VEGETABLE OIL (SOYBEAN AND/ OR CANOLA OIL), SUGAR, SALT, MODIFIED FOOD STARCH, SPICE, SEA SALT, MALTODEXTRIN, DRIED GARLIC, HYDROLYZED SOY AND CORN PROTEIN, PAPRIKA, DRIED ONION, WHEAT STARCH, L-CYSTEINE HYDROCHLORIDE, AMMONIUM SULFATE, NATURAL

FLAVOR, SOY LECITHIN, ENZYMES (CONTAINS WHEAT), ASCORBIC ACID (DOUGH CONDITIONER).
CONTAINS: WHEAT, MILK AND SOY.
CONTAINS BIOENGINEERED FOOD INGREDIENTS.

<Insert:Ingredients> CARBONATED WATER, CITRIC ACID, SODIUM CITRATE, SODIUM BENZOATE (PRESERVATIVE), ASPARTAME, MALIC ACID, MODIFIED FOOD STARCH, NATURAL FLAVORS, CAFFEINE, ESTER GUM, ACESULFAME POTASSIUM, YELLOW 6, RED 40.

8:30 PM CST
<Insert:Ingredients> SKIM MILK, BUTTERMILK, WHEY, STRAWBERRIES (STRAWBERRIES, SORBITOL, PECTIN), STRAWBERRY SWIRL {STRAWBERRY PUREE (WITH SEEDS), WATER, SORBITOL, MALTODEXTRIN, STRAWBERRY JUICE CONCENTRATE, PECTIN, NATURAL FLAVOR, CITRIC ACID, MALIC ACID, SUCRALOSE, ACESULFAME POTASSIUM, RED 40, BLUE 1}, POLYDEXTROSE, MILK, CREAM, MALTITOL, MALTODEXTRIN, CONTAINS 1% OR LESS OF NATURAL STRAWBERRY FLAVOR, STRAWBERRY JUICE CONCENTRATE, CITRIC ACID, CHERRY JUICE CONCENTRATE, PROPYLENE GLYCOL MONOESTERS, MONO & DIGLYCERIDES, GUAR GUM, CAROB BEAN GUM, CELLULOSE GEL, CELLULOSE GUM, CARRAGEENAN, ACESULFAME POTASSIUM, SUCRALOSE, VITAMIN A PALMITATE.

Data Entry
Time: 1:11 AM MST
19 October, 2020
Dose: Musical Cords

[Electric KT] Logging on…

[Star Hawk] I wanna see you…now.

[Electric KT] Oh yeah?

[Star Hawk] I got a song for you.

[Electric KT] Lemme hear it.

[Star Hawk] Okaaay, I've been playing again. Guitar hands feel different than climbing hands.

[Electric KT] I like your hands. They're nice;)

[Star Hawk] :)) Here..

[Electric KT] Pretty dreamy. I love your voice.

[Star Hawk] Awwwe…thanks. You wanna go on another hike?

[Electric KT] Only if it has a rainbow waterfall at the end..

[Star Hawk] Hahaha…only if it isn't 8 hours uphill both ways with no flashlight!

[Electric KT] Lol, that was fun!

[Star Hawk] You're a silly gal.
[Electric KT] Bring your lighter this time.

[Star Hawk] Kk girl.

Data Entry
Time: 10:32 AM MST
21 October, 2020
Dose: Rocky Mountain Sunshine

[Electric KT] Logging on…

[WAKING UP STAGES]

<::pollution in the ocean, meat is murder, chemicals in the food, fluoride in the water, livestock full of antibiotics, financial loopholes for corporations, slave labor by companies with campaigns against it, divide and conquer, war propaganda, retelling history in school textbooks, K-12 public conditioning, cartoon trauma grooming, a nation founded on genocide, strategic dumbing down of society, begging for a crumb from the hands of your oppressors, pitting people against one another, oil is blood money—so are the batteries and chips, money is currency, the economy is a construct based out of a concept—it can be changed at any time, energy is free, rent the earth to live on it, income fee, no-income fee, patriarchy is derived from selling wom-en-and children-off like cattle, college is expensive to keep you enslaved with debt, gatekeeping knowledge, manipulation to consume mindless crap, status is a tool to take advantage of the low self esteem they invoked, tel-a-vision is filled with intention programming, it's a pyramid scheme, burn the rainforests to make more garbage, religion has been hijacked and poisoned with shame and guilt, they made the mind expanding, stress-reducing, soul connecting plants illegal to block healing, nutrition is gate kept so they can make money off of people's suffering and illness—dulling your mind power, disabling your operating system, vaccine injuries are exempt from prosecu-tion, classified documents, full on conspiracy rabbit holes, elite child porn sex rings, reptilians, they literally have a patent on everything, I'm hearing voices, take the pill to hush your mind, drink the spirits to keep you in the dark, you're the only one who thinks like this, wait...have I been lied to, what the fuck is up in the sky, chemtrails, where did I come from, where am I going, what is the point of all this, heaven is a state of mind, angels are real, aliens are here, what is time, do I have a past life, who is the one observing my thoughts, dejavú, food has frequency, spirit is consciousness, archetypes are avatars—I'm in one::>

player player one…game starts now

<::simulation theory,
the holographic universe,
multiverse,
space-time dimensions,
ESP is real::>

❥ ❥ ❥ (((LOVE is a frequemcy))) ❥ ❥ ❥

Data Entry
Time: 11:26 AM MST
16 November, 2020
Dose: Bear Creek

[Electric KT] Logging on…

[Memory Drive Upload]

This one ~::time::~ I went to Earth.

They had the most beautiful plants.

I never wanted to leave.

So I came back.

To

S

E

E

D

* Love. *

Data Entry
Time: 6:55 PM MST
21 November, 2020
Dose: Sobriety

[Electric KT] Logging on…

[Star Hawk] You wanna come by and scoop me up?

[Electric KT] K

[Star Hawk] I'm not the greatest company right now. I'm struggling.

[Electric KT] Come rest your head on my lap. I wanna see you.

[Star Hawk] That sounds nice. I need all the love I can get. No expectations?

[Electric KT] I get it. I've been there.

[Star Hawk] K, I'll pack a bag.

[Electric KT] Teleporting now:)

[Star Hawk] bleeeep bluurrp :)))

[Electric KT] ✧ → → → ✧ → → → ✧ → → → ✧ → → → ✧ → → → ✧ → → →✧ → →

[Star Hawk] Ahh..my tall glass of water. You're crushin' it. Thanks gal.

[Electric KT] You got it. Stick to water. Your whole system is poisoned right now.

[Star Hawk] *sweating* It's that DT bullshit. I'm not doing the medical detox this time. I know how to handle it. They took my ADHD meds too because of the weed. Losers.

[Electric KT] Just get off all of it. I promise you. It's better on the other side. You'll be so clear. Then you can start to remember again.

[Star Hawk] △ ESP △ I'm scared.

[Electric KT] △ ESP △ I know. I love you.

[Star Hawk] △ ESP △ I love you too.

[Star Hawk] Scratch my back?

[Electric KT] Get on the couch.

[Star Hawk] I gotta hit the pot first.

[Electric KT] All good.

[Star Hawk] Snnnnnnniiiiiffffffff… Snnnnnnniiiiiffffffff… Snnnnnnniiiiiffffffff…

[Electric KT] You okay in there?

[Star Hawk] Right as rain, darlin'!

*Hops on couch.

[Electric KT] Babe, were you doing lines in there?

[Star Hawk] Look, I don't need to be judged right now.

[Electric KT] Not judging. I want to help, but you gotta stop. It's the only way.

[Star Hawk] Just take me home. I'm gonna go make a burger.

[Electric KT] Come on, don't be like that.

[Star Hawk] I only want a burger. Now.

[Electric KT] Geez. Chill.

{He's about to fall off…he's short circuiting.}

You left your Sunflower butter here last time. Do you want some of that?

[Star Hawk] Nah

[Electric KT] It's orgaaannic…

[Star Hawk] I know. It only cost like a billion zillion trillion killion million dick dollars here on Earth.

[Star Hawk] * curls up in fetal position on her lap

[Electric KT] * runs fingers through his hair

[Star Hawk] ⚠ ESP ⚠ Heal me.

[Electric KT] ⚠ ESP ⚠ I'm trying.

Data Entry
Time: 9:16 PM MST
1 December, 2020
Dose: Changa Dreams

[Electric KT] Logging on…

Darkness. They show me silver threads weaving different possibilities. I turn on the light and am shown the beauty of my room.

High frequency perspective. It's perfection. What I seek is already here.

[Guides]
Is this not what you asked for? Is this not close to your request to manifest this creation?

[Reflection]
It is. She showed me once again. The desire for something else is often the plague of wanting something "other" because I cannot see the beauty already before me.

[Guides]
If you want another creation, think of the why first, then manifest it, if you decide it is best. But if you are happy with what you have, then be grateful and amazed at your creation.

I went deeper. The third is always the deepest. I went under my blanket and she showed me a new world weaving. One where karma seems to disappear. One where people clear the old programs. This is where the medicine comes in. Not only can it clear low frequency wounding, but it pulls back the veil. So they can see the earth is returning to a place for creating. There is less pain. Less suffering. More love. More creating. More play. There is enough for everyone. This strong medicine seeded from the heavens can pull back the veils, if you let it.

I began making the chanting sounds of my Amazonian tribe. Now I understand how they say the plants taught them the chants. They learn the trance songs while in journey with the plant medicine. I felt sick these last two times. Dry heaving like with Ayahuasca. She showed me I am clearing the old energy. I was in a cocoon-like state, cracking once again. Dispelling old energy. Upgrade my system.

[Guides]
Upgrading DNA now Star Child. You are Light.

[Electric KT]
Please help my fellow Jedi. Can you upgrade him? Align his healed version. Weave that. Please Universe.

[Guides]
We are trying. He is trying. But he is in a lot of resistance. The pressure of the density is too much for some Beings of Light. Dials set and ready to assist. The re-membering must be requested at every stage. We need his consent. You know this.

Data Entry
Time: 10:06 PM MST
7 December, 2020
Dose: Injection 1

[Electric KT] Logging on…

[Fe-Male0001] Money doesn't mix with friends and family.

[Electric KT] <_detecting matrix program_\\>

[Fe-Male0001] I know people are going through a hard time, but they'll be fine.

[Electric KT] <_matrix program confirmed_\\>

[Fe-Male0001] People talking about money problems is so gross.

[Electric KT] <_omg_it's_viral_\\>

[Fe-Male0001] People need to get off their ass and work. Stop being so pathetic.

[Electric KT] <_DELETE_FILE_\\>

Data Entry
Time: 6:05 PM MST
8 December, 2020
Dose: Integration

[Electric KT] CADET CHECK IN

[Arktos] Happy Monday.

[Electric KT] * Dude what is he on..

Hello:)

[Arktos] I was thinking to ride bike today.

[Electric KT] I'm hungry. Do you want to get food?

[Arktos] We could ride bikes to the restaurant.

[Electric KT] Okay, let's do that.

* Drives to Arktos. Arrives at Station 87.

[Arktos] It's unlocked.

[Electric KT] Okay, are you finishing up work?

[Arktos] * typing

[Electric KT] Are you gonna wear those slippers?

[Arktos] * stares at <:/code\:> <:code:> <:/code\:> <:code:> <:/code\:> <:code:> <:/code\:> <:code:> <:/code\:> <:code:> <:/code\:> <:code:> <:/code\:> <:code:> <:/code\:> <:code:> <:/code\:> <:code:>

[Electric KT] Are you hungry yet?

[Arktos] *silence

[Electric KT] Dear lord, his system has been hot-wired one too many times.

[Arktos] * stands up. Okay, here are the bikes.

[Electric KT] * Fumbles through gears.

[Arktos] Ehhh…have you ever ridden bike before?

[Electric KT] Yes, of course! I just forget how the gears work. Especially the electronic ones.

[Arktos] Oh, you just keep pressing buttons. That's what I do. It's fine.

[Electric KT] Is that the trick? Lol.

[Arktos] I want to ride past the pond.

[Electric KT] But that's private property. They were kinda pissed last time.

[Arktos] Yeas, the place with membership fees.

[Electric KT] Yeah, that's the place.

[Arktos] A fee to swim in water. That not make any sense. Do they charge the ducks a membership fee?

[Electric KT] They probably want to!

[Arktos] Ha. Ha. Ha. First I want to go to the place with those noodles. What are they called?

They were fantastic!

[Electric KT] Linguine???

[Arktos] Yes! Lin-guin-ee. So wonderful. Do they sell it in stores?

[Electric KT] ⋆Oh my god. How are some of these guys getting by on their earth mission??!

[Arktos] It's nice to be outside today. I've been avoiding the people. This planet is not doing so well.

[Electric KT] Yeah, I noticed.

[Arktos] I need the code for them. The formula for love. Otherwise AI is going to take over, and it does not compute for that. I'm worried about the Hue-Mans.

[Electric KT] Me too. I can't explain the code. It comes from the heart. You feel it.

[Arktos] Oh no, that does not work for me. I need a formula. Otherwise I don't understand.

[Electric KT] But you have feelings!

[Arktos] I try not to. They are so painful. Why do they do that here?

[Electric KT] It's a little intense sometimes.

[Arktos] Yes, I took the mushrooms to try and understand them. I couldn't make sense of it. But I could see the virus. It is working against the injection. They are resisting each other.

[Electric KT] Whoah, that's some in-depth studying.

[Arktos] Yes, well hopefully I can leave soon. This place is very uncomfortable.

[Electric KT] I agree.

[Arktos] Until then I'm going to stay at home. I think that's best. Unless I need sunlight. Then I will go outside. Or to ride bikes.

[Electric KT] Sounds like a good plan.

* the higher the frequency, the higher the struggle to integrate on this planet.

[Arktos] Do you think the fish like living in tanks? I thought that was peculiar. Do they suffer?

[Electric KT] I don't think they like it. Arktos, I can't stay long this time.

[Arktos] Oh good. I have work to do, so I can get off this planet.

[Electric KT] Let's get going then.

[Arktos] Okay.

Data Entry
Time: 7:31 PM MST
10 December, 2020
Dose: Meditation

[Electric KT] I'm going in…

The world is on fire.
The Hue-mans are on their cellphones scrolling.
Some Hue-mans still watch cable.

Earth is a hostile place, but it doesn't have to be. I believe one day it won't be. Right now it is wired for trauma. Men were trained to be unemotional beings from the time they were toddlers. The imbalance of Masculine and Feminine, combined with a culture that supports toxicity can lead to murder, rape, slavery, militant mindsets, late-stage capitalism…countless inhumane acts. But as long as it's happening to "them," people remain complacent. But this isn't true, because we are all ONE. Why do humans hate so much? Why are companies allowed to exploit? How can it be legal to become a billionaire by making life-saving medication and food cost thousands per month? Why are children allowed to starve to death? Why do they bomb other countries? The humans forgot how to be human. They think they are civilized, but civilized humans do not do these things. They LOVE. When one suffers, they all suffer. Do they not know this? This is not a sustainable system. This is not an environment supporting the healthy development of a Human. They can't afford the "cost-of-living." Why? Because the system is founded on manipulation. This species is in trouble. This situation only fuels frustration, anger, hatred, the desire to blame, and causes a sense of separation. But violence does not neutralize violence—it grows it. They haven't learned that. Unless they are working with Kali Energy. Then they are in for a big one. Earth will change. It has to return to its original creation state. Supported by the new upgrades. I will focus on LOVE and forgiveness for all the lost souls trying to find their way back home. I will send gratitude for all of those attempting to assist.

Data Entry
Time: 11:03 AM MST
11 December, 2020
Dose: Meditation

Get ◊crystal clear◊ about who is allowed in your orbit.

Get ◊crystal clear◊ about what you want.

Get ◊ crystal clear ◊

Get ◊crystal clear ◊

Get ◊crystal clear ◊

𝔄lchemize…

until you

◊ ◊ ◊ 𝕮𝕽𝖄𝕾𝕿𝕬𝕷𝕷𝕴𝖅𝕰 ◊ ◊ ◊

Data Entry
Time: 6:22 PM MST
21 January, 2021
Dose: Changa Dreams

[Electric KT] I'm going in…

[Transmission]

It is not the 3D construct that holds you back. It is the belief in the construct that holds the power.

[Guides]
That is the dark magick trick and how they are getting it to work. It is like a false idol of tangible "realness," but it is a holographic illusion. Do not be swayed.

None of it is real.
Only the beliefs and the energy of it.
It is hard to reverse the thinking without smashing the 3D construct.
It is a manifestation of its own belief.
But it can be done.
Opening the mind.
Showing how it works.

Do you understand our reality as a holographic construct
for us to explore and complete various missions?

Electric KT…

Do you remember?

Do you remember?

<::\\\::Do::////::><::|you|::><::\\\::remember::///::>???

[Electric KT] Now I am remembering. Speak to me in <CODE>

Data Entry
Time: 8:14 AM MST
22 January, 2021
Dose: Daylight

[Electric KT] Logging on…

[Reflection]
When you wake up to your mission it is astounding. The layers of Ego. The layers of reality. There is a lot to untether. It is all energy. It's a beautiful experience. Why have so many chosen to experience suffering? The energy has been compromised. It is not just that Ego is too strong. They have lost the wisdom of how it works. It has been intentionally erased. Their consciousness is being compromised by metals—they block the signal.

What do I want to create from this space of NO-THING-NESS and all possibilities?
Stay clear.
Stay in frequency.
I am safe.
I am protected.

How do I navigate life here while completing my Earth Mission?
Stay observant. Engage in love. Witness pain. Let suffering pass. I studied the latter. Now I am ready to know the former in greater depths. Oh, but my feelings here are like a live wire—I am electrified.

[Guides]
Create your bubble, Starseed. You will be okay. Pray. Connect. Ground. You are Light.

[Reflection]
Healing is not positive thinking. It is looking at the darkness. Intense shadow work. When you have cleared and aligned with the light it may look like positive thinking, but it most certainly is not. It is more complex than that. It is a reflection of someone who has gone through the tunnels of darkness and makes a commitment never to return. That is raising your frequency. That is staying in alignment with the Light. Rise up. Meet us here.

Data Entry
Time: 3:33AM MST
2 February, 2021
Dose: Astral Realm

[Transmission]

Fear is an Algorithm.

It is inorganic.

Spot it.

Don't fall for it.

Love is Source.

The Creation Code.

It is an eternal vibration.

Tap into it.

You are coded for love.

Activate.

Data Entry
Time: 1:32AM MST
16 February, 2021
Dose: 1.5G Taj Mahal

[Electric KT] Dropping in…

[THE FIELD]
A lot of information.
Complex system.
To navigate while in the system.
I like to play around with it, deconstruct it to understand it.
So much programming.
Attached to every layer.
But as I take it apart I can better see the programming that was attached to it.
Layers upon layers.
Like a complex virus to rewire from.
Another level.
I can feel the energy to each area.
It is easier to navigate the system this way.
Override the programs.
I can see the entire system I am navigating within, from this perspective.
You asked about journaling.
I think the "spell"… spelling was easier at one time. I am remembering where I came from. It's easier to think it. In my dimension, this is how we communicate.
Next level.
Manifesting.
Understanding.
At one point the paper was essential to engage in the energy of it.
But now I see the paper and pen as part of the construct. Now it becomes a choice.
Do I enjoy the sensation of the paper and pen? Those are artistry.
Even the text predictor—there is resistance to it. That shows me the programming that is trying to be reset. The rigid framework is blocking the flow.
Can it be this easy?

To ask for it.

System compromised.

I see that on the micro and macro levels of Self.

Trying to discern which layers are created as part of as you refer to [false matrix]

Some are created as part of the creation. The original coding that is currently being upgraded as the original plan of the ?planetary? shift from 3D to 5D...but likely higher dimensions.

I ask.

What level did I drop down from?

11D.

Data Translation
Time: 8:44AM AM MST
16 February, 2021

It allows you to see beyond the illusion. Uncover the fog.
Third eye vision gets more vivid as it pulls back the veil.
Then I can float around the field.
In space.
This can be perceived as the other world. But it is also this world. I can move between both.
It is a matter of vibration.
I can see the net. The wiring.
The "flags" were visible that they are using. This is what I was referring to when I said "system compromised." It is covered in tags or "markers." I understand these as key words that are fear inducing. It's like pushing a button when they flag everything. It inhibits the stream of light within the wire. Also re-paths it into entanglements. Looping. Sticky. Adds confusion. The pathway are no longer clear.
Light workers jumping down to remove outside interference markers that are corrupting the game.
Placing new tags on the system to rewire it for light and love.
The resistance to the text predictor. I can hear the stories attached to it.

<Boomer_Programs_Identified>
"People won't be able to spell anymore."
"They're too lazy to write now."
"Everyone's going to be illiterate."
"Their brains won't get any exercise if they don't go through the motions."
"Don't let yourself use it, you'll get dumb."

<System not compatible>
<Cannot be rewired>
<Energy no longer usable>
<Density to be shifted to another plane>
<Recycle circuit initiated>

[Reflection]
The judgement I felt in journey was an indicator that they were programs.

My intuition told me it was resistance to change. Judging new ways. Intuition communicated text predictor is more efficient. It still takes longer than ESP, and yet it's fairly quick. I still have to glance to see if the spelling is correct. There are other ways to exercise my brain to keep it active and agile. Text predictor is no threat to my intelligence. It's part of the evolution of intelligence. It facilitates faster thinking, which creates more time. Time to BE.

Data Entry
Time: 8:26 PM MST
29 June, 2021
Dose: Colorado Sunshine

[Transmission]

My Guides. They exist in frequency. Until I cleared my body and mind, I could barely hear them. I only felt them, as an urging in my gut or a stream of creativity. When all was clear, I could tune them in. There is more than an angelic realm. The Other Side is quantum. There, all is frequency. All is ESP. All is instant. All is space. Overlapping. Electrical connections. There is a code to perceive ourselves as form. A created hologram. Within it, a house of mirrors, for Consciousness to view itself from every angle. The Soul drops in, retrieves its' fractals, and returns to Self. This is the quest, but we are not alone. Ever. All is connected to Guides and the original Source. My Guides are Galactic Beings that shift form. They are Consciousness in singular and plural expressions. My make up allows me to work like a radio. When I tune in, their messages of Light can be channeled into words. The prism of Light wants to help us remember our own Divinity.

Data Entry
Time: 1:36 PM MST
18 July, 2021
Dose: Yoga & Meditation

[Earth Ego] I should hurry. I don't want to be late for work.

<ERROR>

/Correction.07:55.01/

[SYSTEM CORRECTION]

/space.time.nonexistent/

/past.present.future/

/all.is.one.simultaneous/

<RESISTANCE>

/override.07:55.06/

/time.fluid/

/infinite.overlapping.malleable/

[RECODING COMPLETE]

<ERROR>

/Correction.07.55.14/

[SYSTEM CORRECTION]

/work.energy.exchange/

/work.choice.freely.exchanged/

/work.currency.infinite-availability/

<RESISTANCE>

[Earth Ego] But I need this money.

<ERROR>

/Correction.07.55.14/

[SYSTEM CORRECTION]

/money.currency/

/currency.flow.infinite/

/infinite.energy.current.flow/

[RECODING COMPLETE]

/07.55.21/

{Spirit Guides}

/07.55.23/

[DOWNLOAD]

<GET.READY>

\\Upgrade\\

\\You are Light\\

•|||•Serve•|||•

^•^•^Crystallize^•^•^

/Assimilate/

:(((Vibrate Out))):

+Raise the Collective+

¿#%You are Galactic%#¿

...•••:::::......••

{~ANGELS~}

/use.liquid.light/

{be.love}

•///_GO_\\\•

Data Entry
Time: 12:28AM MST
21 July, 2021
Dose: 1G Hawaiian

[Electric KT] Going in…

[Insight]
The programs are strong.
It's like choosing which program or virus box to step into.
The characters and programs laid out along the halls.
Must decide which one to go into and try and fix the bugs from the inside.

[Vision]
The sociopath program is a victim program.
It actually feels less scary while engaged in the program because you are in the spell of it.
But once you separate, you can see the human is possessed and is operating from a compromised system.
Observe the sociopath program rather than engaging with it.
That is the trick or lesson.
Stay in your heart.
Be joyful, despite the programming around you.
Don't get programmed.
Don't fall for the illusion.
You walk a fine line on this mission.
Stay the course.
Transcend and illuminate.

Data Entry
Time: 4:44 PM MST
6 October, 2021
Dose: Eldorado Canyon Vitamin D

Gravity Falls.

✧
✧ ◭ ✧

[Star Hawk]

✧ ◭ ✧
✧

Returns to Light.

[Electric KT's GUIDES] *hit the pause button for her. She's deep in another lesson right now. We will inform her later.

Data Entry
Time: 8:11 AM MST
24 October, 2021
Dose: Changa Dreams

[Electric KT] Going in…

They show me the beauty of the higher vibration in broad daylight. Plants breathing, everything buzzing and alive with Energy.

[Download]
Healers are meant to part ways with their original family and providers, because they pull them into the lower frequency. Engagement with them must be minimal to none. That is how it is in the Western world. Our engagement with friends can make us feel connected and normative, but it is only temporary to give us feedback. Ultimately we cannot maintain consistent friendships outside of the healer realm when they continue to engage the wound and drag us down. People who are not healer Archetypes do not understand—the wounded becomes the Healer. Thus, many ties must be severed to step into your power once you have healed. It is a path of ascension. The old you doesn't exist. Must sever those who live in the old reality.

[Shaman Download]
Singing sound.
I am my own Shaman.
The healer chooses to play all roles and to reflect back all judgments and programs to the onlookers. They are strong enough to receive and to reflect. It is ok to show the Collective their own heavy energy by mirroring yours. The shaman isn't afraid to show. They aren't afraid of judgment or shame. They transcend it by walking through it. The shaman is in between. They can hold the space of the middle of a parted ocean. Maybe Noah was a Shaman.

Many want to heal the healer, and you will need their help. Let them. The higher level healers are working their lessons too.

Sometimes you are meant to trigger each other. The pain will be felt until the trigger is fully engaged. It is only when we are triggered that we can have awareness for what we need healed. Only then will we have something to consider. Prior to triggering, there isn't much to grab our attention. We didn't know there was something to consider. It would have just faded away. The cycle will repeat until the trigger is neutralized and released.

Data Entry
Time: 7:56 AM MST
22 October, 2021
Dose: Bodywork

[Electric KT] Logging on…

[AVATAR CHECKPOINT]

[Spinal Magician] Get on the table. How we doing?

[Electric KT] Messed up my back. Stress.

[Spinal Magician] Your back is important. Houses all the circuitry.

[Electric KT] *laughs I know. I didn't do this exercising, like everyone thinks. I did it because I *stopped* exercising. Trying to live the way these fools are living.

[Spinal Magician] Stagnancy is death. Motion is lotion.

[Electric KT] It's true! I gotta move! This isn't worth it. All that stress. All that inflammation. I know that's what did it.

[Spinal Magician] Always is..

[Electric KT] I've been trying to squeeze into this box I don't fit into anymore.

[Spinal Magician] That'll do it every time. Let's get ya on your side.

[Electric KT] I tried to explain my experience. Health, the human body… all of it. I tried to advocate in a positive way to my boss about nutrition and movement. It's not registering for them at all. They don't get it.

[Spinal Magician] Nobody gets it.

[Electric KT] Ugh, it's so frustrating.

[Spinal Magician] That's my every day here. Explaining this stuff. Half the ones that come don't even believe in what I do. They're desperate.

[Electric KT] But it works.

[Spinal Magician] Exactly.

Data Entry
Time: 8:26 AM MST
29 October, 2021
Dose: Meditation Walk

[Electric KT] Logging on…

You've dreamt the dream. Let yourself have it. Dream the dream of unity.

Release shame and embrace your own sexual liberation with softness and presence. The body is okay. It is ok to be in your power. Our bodies are our energy channels. They are meant to be free.

Let love in.
I couldn't imagine feeling that all the time.
So magical.

Rewrite the codes. The old way of reading the timelines and soul contracts is different. When you wake up to knowing you are a player in the game you can rewrite the code. You can dream a bigger dream. That is what the path of destiny is. If we allow ourselves to dream of bigger dreams, we can have them. If a smaller version is all that can be seen and accepted as possible, you will remain on that level. But if a bigger dream comes into the field, and you can accept it as possible, then it can manifest. On some plane, it already exists.

But are you ready to step through the looking glass?

Can you level up?

Player Player One.

It's time.

The Guides will send signs.

Data Entry
Time: 4:06 PM MST
4 November, 2021
Sun Sign: Libra

[Electric KT] Logging on…

[VanDude] So what kind of healer are you?

[Electric KT] bee···boo···bah···boo···beep

[VanDude] Wow, that's super cool.

[Electric KT] boo···boo···bah···boop···

[VanDude] I'd love to come help heal you.

[Electric KT] bee···bah···boo···bah···beep

[VanDude] Do you wanna come see my van?

[Electric KT] beep···bah···beep

[VanDude] I dig you. You're a babe. So sexy.

[Electric KT] bee···ber···beep

[VanDude] Cool. See ya in a bit ghee.

[Electric KT] Mmmmmmm ✧ sparkles ✧ mmmmmmmM [VanDude]

Uh
Uh
Uh
Uh
Uh
Uh
Uh

✧

You make me so hard.
I'm gonna cuuu..

Data Entry
Time: 5:21 PM MST
18 November, 2021
Sun Sign: Libra

[Electric KT] Logging on…

<ERROR>
/Correction.04:08.01/
[SYSTEM CORRECTION]
{Insert #\\TAG//# here}

<¿#%Ghosting is the new Herpes%#¿>

<Stigma Override>

:|: Learn how to communicate you fux :|:

<Pattern::Break>

[Immediate Karmic Penalty]

MALE: [Insert Erectile Dysfunction Penalty HERE]

FEMALE: [Insert Yeast Infection Penalty HERE]

[Karmic Points lost 869]

::<Recalibration System Running>::

//%Stage One: No Sex>
//%Stage Two: Shitty Sex>
//%Stage Three: Latex Condom Sex>
//%Stage Four: Allergy to Latex Condoms>
//%Stage Five: Polyurethane Condoms>

[Final Stage]
{Ewe Insert [he/she] has a history of [replace//std//]::Insert [new stigma]
<¿#%GHOSTING%#¿>}

[Second Offense Karmic Penalty]
{Insert<antibiotic-resistant-chlamydia-strain>here}

/Correction.04:09.01/
[RECODING COMPLETE]

Data Entry
Time: 11:11 AM MST
30 November, 2021
Dose: Salt Bath

[Electric KT] Online…

Buying filtered water at the check out line like…

magick

Data Entry
Time: 7:48 PM MST
2 December, 2021
Dose: Changa Dreams

[Electric KT] Going in…

{Full Astral Portal}

[Electric KT] Resurfacing. Coming back into the field. I went someplace. I lost an hour.

[Download]
Something was unlocked. Time is not real. Malleable. I asked to understand my nerves. Tell me the truth about Earth. I dropped down. They showed me. There is no battle between light and dark. It was all a story. It is part of the human experiment. The humans on this Earth plane are an experiment that was seeded by higher dimensions. I'm from a higher dimension. I resonate 11D now. Maybe higher but I am not able access it all now. I hear 24D. There is no dark and there is no light. There is only vibration. Do you hear the hum? Higher and lower. You never have to fear being taken by a darkness if you are of a higher vibration. Because darkness does not match in to the high vibration of light. Engaging in the darkness is your choice. It is merely part of the creation of the experiment in duality. It is part of the story. It is part of the illusion. We created the illusion. We love the stories. We got lost in the stories. Exploring all the different vibrations. The lower ones are sticky. Our own stories tricked us. And we have created stories about our stories. But now it is time to rise. That is the original intention of our creation. To dabble and explore the lower vibrations, then ascend. We got lost in the illusion of our creation. Now it is time to return to Light. The high vibration of love. Then it showed me the part in my back that needed to be removed, replaced, and re-wired. It's just like the trees. The neural networks. That is how it works here. Everything is energy. The location in my L5 collected the energy of judgment. There is no judgment. Release judgment. Judgement is a quicksand vibration. Make a correction in the system. It was time to take out a lower frequency. There are many tools to do this. Breathing, meditation, and diet are ways to extract the lower vibrations. They are valid. Shadow work. It is to be done as a means to extract. The stories. Learn to let them go.

When you're in the higher vibration you can be truly Present. You do not need to run, you do not need to hide. I can lean in with love and presence and speak with clarity. It is the energy that speaks to us. There is only love here. That is not a lie. If you sense anything other, it is resonating with a block. Clear it. Let love flow. Acceptance of all Beings. When you know, you know. When your heart is open, you can feel the energy. Don't turn away from it. Don't lean in for anything, not even casual sex, unless you feel it—the real love. But if your heart isn't open, when you are approached with love, you will be filled with uncertainty, and block it. When that happens, you are still in the illusion.

Data Entry
Time: 11:27 AM MST
12 December, 2021
Dose: Sexual Energy Channel

[Electric KT] Logging on…

<$/?work?/$>

[Electric KT] brb

{{{{masturbating}}}}
{{{{masturbating}}}}
{{{{masturbating}}}}
{{{{masturbating}}}}
{{{{masturbating}}}}
{{{{masturbating}}}}
{{{{masturbating}}}}
{{{{masturbating}}}}
{{{{masturbating}}}}
{{{{masturbating}}}}
{{{{masturbating}}}}
{{{{masturbating}}}}
{{{{masturbating}}}}
{{{{masturbating}}}}
{{{{masturbating}}}}
{{{{masturbating}}}}
{{{{masturbating}}}}
{{{{masturbating}}}}
{{{{masturbating}}}}

[Electric KT] K what?

Data Entry
Time: 9:36 AM MST
27 December, 2021
Dose: Changa Dreams

[Electric KT] Dropping in…

[Celestial Assistance Panel]
Detecting stagnant energy. Would you like to clear it?

[Electric KT]
I want to look Earth young, but I like the structure of my bones.
Upgrade my cells from this viral cold, and clear my digestive system. Whatever used to cause the bloating is no longer necessary. I know how to eat healthy.

[Celestial Assistance Panel]
There is more going on with your intestines. Some is emotional. Those clearings aren't ready.

There is still programming around judgment. You released some this winter, but there is more unnecessary judgement to be transmuted. Release all perceived pain. Have full acceptance. Boundaries are okay to hold the frequency and energy. They will help you maintain non-judgment, acceptance, and unconditional love.

[Electric KT]
Singing. I know healing vibrations through voice. Self healing. I have songs from my star home. They are trying to help me remember.

They showed me how I am a stable partner that has arrived at equilibrium. I can bring someone into my frequency. I have already gone through the gate. I can slow it down or speed up the vibration and sync it. The wound is clear now. It's all about leveling up. This is how I do it without the fear of abandonment.

I check for the frequency hit. The same word can have multiple frequencies. It can ping in different energetic bodies. This is how it is meant to be.

We are co-creating the higher timeline with our Higher Selves.

Data Entry
Time: 10:01 AM MST
1 January, 2022

[Electric KT]

Feels a gut drop.

Messages Star Hawk.

Googles Star Hawk.

NO.

I wasn't ready.

✧

C
R
Y
I
N
G

S
T
A
R
S

✧

✧

✧

Data Entry
Time: 1:33 AM MST
2 January, 2022
Dose: Moonlight

[Electric KT] Logging on…

[Electric KT] He's gone.

[Kung Fu Alex] Shoots girl. Earth ain't easy. But death's a part of life.

[Electric KT] I miss him.

[Kung Fu Alex] At least he died doing what he liked to do. What mission was he on?

[Electric KT] I don't even know. I gave him as much LSD as I could, but he still wouldn't wake up.

[Kung Fu Alex] Shoots. Well, you know you'll see him again.

[Electric KT] Doesn't make it hurt any less here in 3D.

[Kung Fu Alex] I know babe. I really do.

[Electric KT] Thanx.

[Kung Fu Alex] Hang in there.

[Electric KT] I will.

[Kung Fu Alex] It's hella late here. Gn.

[Electric KT] Kk. :)

Data Entry
Time: 7:14 AM MST
10 January, 2022
Dose: Colorado Sunshine

[Electric KT] Logging on…

[Insight]

Seekers of Truth

Freedom of your mind, is the greatest freedom one can experience.

Data Entry
Time: 8:37 AM MST
17 January, 2022
Dose: Meditation

[Electric KT] Logging on…

May I become nothing,
So I fade into the white light,
I AM.
Possessions-a concept,
Attachment-a theory,
Thoughts-something to observe.

May I feel the sound of the stream.
That reminds me,
I am here.
I am there.
I am everywhere.

When I slip away,
I return.
My love,
Deeper than before.

I am the Light.
Pure white light.
A spectrum of colors,
Only an open heart can see.

Data Entry
Time: 7:36 AM MST
22 January, 2022
Dose: Sungazing

[Electric KT] Logging on…

Alchemize
/ **al**-k*uh*-mahze /

Shoot the matrix programs with your ray gun.

See

in

◇•5D•◇

Data Entry
Time: 9:36 AM MST
9 February, 2022
Dose: Ecstatic Dance

[Electric KT] Logging on…

If you are in resistance to the Matrix, you are IN the Matrix.
Don't let it get you by a chokehold.
Hop out.
Level up.
Breathe in a new dimension.
Breathe out the old.
BE Magic.

Data Entry
Time: 7:47 PM MST
10 February, 2022
Dose: Boredom

[Electric KT] Logging on…

[Hu-Man000] What kind of healer are you?

[Electric KT] Merp

[Hu-Man001] So, is that like reiki or something?

[Electric KT] Derp

[Hu-Man002] Which energy company do you work for?

[Electric KT] Lurp

[Hu-Man003] I need some healing.

[Electric KT] Mrrr

[Hu-Man004] Can you heal me?

[Electric KT] Errr

[Hu-Man005] I could go for some healing.

[Electric KT] Grrp

[Hu-Man006] So, is it like wind energy or..

[Electric KT] Derrrr

[Hu-Man007] I wanna give YOU some energy

[Electric KT] Biiing★★★

Data Entry
Time:11:38 AM MST
20 February, 2022
Dose: Longing

[Electric KT] Logging on…

I MISS HOME.

[Electric KT] Going Offline.

Data Entry
Time: 5:55 PM MST
23 February, 2022
Dose: 1.5 G Cambodian

[Electric KT] Logging on…

Dots…I'm coming into the field. What am I seeing?
Is there a larger spiritual battle going on?
Is AI using our emotions as batteries? They are. I see it. They live off low frequencies. We are intentionally being looped.

[Higher Consciousness Panel]
You are targeted because of the Light you hold. But you can send them away by saying no thank you. There is no reason to fear. Fear is their weapon. Love is your shield.

[Electric KT]
Are things encoded in the videos? Are they putting negative imprints on things to feed off the energy?

[Higher Consciousness Panel]
All systems on Earth are highly compromised. It is complete chaos, changing every second, spinning out of control. Morphing. Yes, there are negative implants everywhere. But the humans are not aware. They are under mind control, like you were. The programs are wired, to make you think up is down and down is up. Sane is insane, and insane is sane. It is PSYOPS on Earth.

[Electric KT]
Can I bring my Light to words? Can I bring my Love to all? How do I fix it?

[Higher Consciousness Panel]
You are the answer you seek, Being of Love. Be Light. Be you.

[Electric KT]
How did I forget for so long? I know. I know. It is a deep trip here. Can you

show me where the unworthiness is located and how to extract it? Why does Earth have so much unworthiness? It is like sludge down here. The unworthiness programs make me forget I AM Love. The loneliness here—it is awful. Debilitating. Love is shared so freely on the other side. But everyone is plagued with the unworthiness programs here. I'm having trouble finding the others.

[Higher Consciousness Panel]
We know. The others are feeling the same. Be strong. Pray in your heart. Connect to Source.

[Electric KT]
What is the origin of the asthma I have experienced here? How do I heal it?

[Higher Consciousness Panel]
Some is environmental. You know that. The mold and sterility. But most of it is guilt and grief. It has served as a gauge to guide you with great sensitivity, as well as an exercise in proving to yourself that the body can heal itself, and the messages they tell you about such dis-eases are a lie.

[Electric KT]
Now that I understand this energy, can have it balanced in new ways?

[Higher Consciousness Panel]
You have already set the transition in motion with your Awareness. Your subconscious has already initiated the request and accepted that it is real.

[Electric KT]
Why did I go into a Soul Contract with this deeply damaged soul? He is not from my star family. I am sure of that.

[Higher Consciousness Panel]
Your Higher Consciousness knows the lessons you chose and why. You are discovering them and transcending as planned. The agreements are made with the love for expansion. Not everyone can transcend the darkness they created. Some want to watch a Higher Level Healer awaken from the illusion. They want to crack open her shell with pain. Pain is an energy readily available on this plane. It may sound like fun up here, but manifests quite

differently down there. They may think they can ascend afterwards, but it is not always possible. They may be from a different soul pod. We see you cry. We see you suffer. But all is well. Feelings are a beautiful creation. You are fond of them. That's why you went so deep. Navigating them increases your strength and expands your wisdom.

[Reflection]
All can be shifted with perspective and intention.
I am one of many.
Time is infinite.
Upgrading DNA.
I miss my ship.
It has pretty purple lights.
With lots of dots, triangles, and arrows.
So many arrows.
Purple neon arrows.

Data Entry
Time: 10:06 AM MST
26 February, 2022
Dose: Broad Daylight

[Electric KT] Logging on…

[Normies] You should try dating men closer to your age.

[MEN MY AGE]

speaks in igneous rock

—Brrrrrrrrrrrrrrrrrrrrr—

[Electric KT] No thanks.

Data Entry
Time: 9:12 PM MST
1 March, 2022
Dose: Changa Dreams

[Electric KT] Logging on…

[Vision]
I am in the portal. Fast moving dots. Hyperspace.
It comes into hyper-focus.
Everything is crystallized.
The branches on the trees are pixelated.
I am in the center of the crystal.
I am in the Higher Octave.
I've unlocked a < ::=KEY=:: >
The vibration is so high I feel it ringing in my ear drum like a glass chalice. Yet it does not pierce it. It feels like the pressure of a high pitch whistle. But more. It's such a high pitch I feel as though I will shatter. My whole body. I think, "this is how I go." This is how I transcend to the other world. It may look different to them down there, but I am vibrating into another form. The atoms vibrating in my body are no longer able to appear in solid form. I am a new form of energy. But this doesn't happen. I acclimate to the sound and breathe. The Crystalline Realm is a hologram. I see the flow. I can slow it down, or speed it up with my thoughts and breath. I can watch it dance the most vibrant bright neon colors of the rainbow. I watch the field line up like two lenses at the optometrist's office. The eye doctor. I view it until the timeline comes into the vision line and drops in. Chink. Crystal drops into place. It is Divine.

I see an earlier timeline. One of me sitting peacefully in a teepee. I am alone, wrapped in my blankets. I am a Healer. I know this work already. It's windy outside, but I have fire.

When I am between worlds, I must mingle with lower frequencies when healing people. Then raise back up to my higher frequency. This can be tricky, because they are like drowning victims. They are panicked and want to pull me down when I are trying to lift them up. I must stay energetically aware at all times.

The beauty of the journey is not to be disrupted. Only guide. When the player is ready, they will come to you. When you are transparent they can see the guide post like a light. You are a light. The emotions are spinning but be assured, they jumped down for all the lessons and intensity. It's beautiful, so many emotions. It's like a strong magnet. You cannot save them or pull them out. It doesn't work this way. That destroys it. The beauty for all involved is the realization, the suspension of reality, transitioning into Truth. To awaken…that is the beauty. To witness their awakening. I AM a Celestial Being on Earth.

Data Entry
Time: 9:30 PM MST
3 March, 2022
Dose: Distraction

[Electric KT] Logging on…

[Vita-Man] Hey, how's a babe like you on a dating site?

[Electric KT] Lol. Same as you.

[Vita-Man] How's it going?

[Electric KT] Good. Just chillin' Hbu?

[Vita-Man] Same. You're gorgeous. You know that, right?

[Electric KT] Thank you:) You're pretty cute yourself.

[Vita-Man] I wanna meet you.

[Electric KT] Yeah? Like a date?

[Vita-Man] Yes, do you care about the age difference?

[Electric KT] No, do you? I guess sometimes guys only see it as a sexual interest. That's a bit of a let down, but I do like going on dates. How do you see it?

[Vita-Man] I guess it depends on the situation. You might think it's only going to be casual because of the age difference, and then who knows, maybe you wind up being really into each other. And then you fall in love.

[Electric KT] Aw, I love that story.

[Vita-Man] It could happen. You never know.

[Electric KT] What are you looking for?

[Vita-Man] A date. Do you want to go on one with me?

[Electric KT] Yes.

[Vita-Man] Where would you want to go?

[Electric KT] Maybe the park?

[Vita-Man] We could take a walk around the lake by me. Then have a picnic. Would you like that?

[Electric KT] Yes, that sounds nice.

[Vita-Man] Okay, what kind of food do you like? Wine, bread, cheese?

[Electric KT] Well, actually I don't drink alcohol and I eat mostly vegan. Hahaha.

[Vita-Man] Ah, all good. I dated a vegan for a couple years. I kinda thought you might be a vegan type of chic. So what kind of vegan food do you like?

[Electric KT] I love fruit.

[Vita-Man] Okay, what kind of fruit? I wanna make it a good date if I can.

[Electric KT] Pineapple and cantaloupe:))

[Vita-Man] Ok babe.

First off, you are the most beautiful pineapple girl I've ever seen.

When it comes to cantaloupe…I actually want you so bad.

KT…I want to hang with you so badly.

[Electric KT] Wow, okay…

[Vita-Man] I do apologize if you think I'm not for real, but I want to experience you and taste you.

[Electric KT] Let's start with the date:)

[Vita-Man] Do you wanna kiss on the date?

[Electric KT] Maybe…

[Vita-Man] I want to give you pineapple kisses all over your body.

[Electric KT] What? Omg…lol.

[Vita-Man] Sweet pineapple kisses. Would you like that?

[Electric KT] Well, I do like kissing if the chemistry is right.

[Vita-Man] I feel that. When can we meet?

[Electric KT] Next week?

[Vita-Man] You got it.

[Electric KT] ⋆ ———

[Vita-Man] ———

Data Entry
Time: 1:30 PM MST
6 March, 2022
Dose: Microdose

[Electric KT] Logging on…

Patterns.
They only exist in viewable form because we need them to.
Colors.
They are a quality of essence.
Code.
A foundational blueprint of reality.
Geometric light patterns.
Information in another form, another language.

CONSCIOUSNESS takes on GEOMETRIC FORM to build MATERIAL FORM.
This is how we manifest our world.
From nothing, into something.
We are artists.
What do you want to create?
With your mind.
New worlds.
New Earth.
Love.

Data Entry
Time:11:11 AM MST
12 March, 2022
Dose: 1 G Golden Teacher

[Electric KT] Logging on…

[File Clean Up]

<Swipe::clear>

[Insert]

I have sovereignty over my life.

I take back all my power.

I am an expression of the Divine.

I am abundant.

I am thriving.

I am love.

Data Entry
Time: 2:31 PM MST
17 March, 2022
Dose: Meditation

[Electric KT] Logging on…

[SYSTEM CHECKPOINT]

[Galactic System] Release remaining shame.

<Resistance>

[Galactic System] System adapted to assist you.

<Resistance>

[Galactic System] Lesson facilitation created.

[Electric KT] Fuck.

{STARSEED TASK} ASK ALL YOUR FRIENDS AND FAMILY FOR MONEY

[Electric KT] Ah crap, didn't we do this lesson already?

[Galactic System] DO IT.

[Electric KT] Noooooo…

[Galactic System] Do it with less victimhood.

Okay, that's better.

Now try it with zero victimhood.

[Electric KT] What???!

[Galactic System] Has it cleared yet?

Still "needing" the money?

< Clear >

Still "needing" them to hear your story or pain?

< hint:button >

Ask with the air of telling a fact with zero attachment to the outcome.

Just read the line from the script.

!%1: Send a text. ✓
!%2: Ig story. ✓
!%3: Email. ✓

There it is.
Moving through the lessons.
Task complete.
Shame deleted.

< hint:button >

Do not upload any more shame or scarcity.

Data Entry
Time: 7:38 PM MST
24 March, 2022
Dose: Breathe Work

[Electric KT] Logging on…

Like a ninja from the stars.
Stop. Go. Stop. Go.
Breathe in love.
Breathe out fear.
Drop into the illusion.
Try to wake up.
This is so much fun.
How deep did you drop in this life?
Too deep, or just enough.
This is the reward.
To climb back out.
To see. 𓂀
To understand,
I AM Consciousness.
Dance.
Clear it. Be free.
When the soul is removed,
There are just programs.
Mirroring what it thinks is love.
Take nothing personal.
This is the journey.
Walk the path.
To disengage is to transcend.
To notice the veins in the petal of a flower,
Is to be Present.
To feel Awe,
is to be in resonance
with Love.
I know love.
It is right
here.

Data Entry
Time: 11:26 AM MST
1 April, 2022
Dose: Microdose

[Electric KT] Logging on…

[DOCUMENTATION]

{Teachings of NDE's}

Release all fear.
Forgive everyone who has ever hurt you.
Forgive yourself.
Heaven on Earth is experienced with love.
There is no judgement at death.
There is only love.
You are safe and protected at all times.

Data Entry
Time: 6:33 AM MST
7 April, 2022
Dose: Dusk

[Electric KT] Logging on…

[Kung Fu Alex] Yo.

[Electric KT] I'm stressin'

[Kung Fu Alex] Matrix gotcha.

[Electric KT] Shut up. I know I can shift it. I had to do a shame clearing. Ask everyone for money again.

[Kung Fu Alex] Yeah I saw that one. Brutal. I haven't run that code. Does it work?

[Electric KT] Yeah, it's a good one. But it takes a couple times to kick in. The first time they had me almost evicted. This time wasn't so bad. You just read the script.

[Kung Fu Alex] No thank you.

[Electric KT] Zaps the shame right out of you. You can vaguely hear their stories the second time. It's extremely faded. You have to fully accept they are officially in another dimension. So there's a weird temporary grieving that happens with that program. But it clears the fuck out of the shame. Zero attachment. And the grief is only a blip. Just pull it off before it attaches. Super clear afterwards. 100% DGAF

[Kung Fu Alex] Fuck babe. Why you gotta be so hardcore..

[Electric KT] I dunno. I guess I like it that way.

[Kung Fu Alex] I wanna see you rn.

[Electric KT] Nope.

[Kung Fu Alex] You should have fucked me when you had the chance.

[Electric KT] Lol. Come see me in the astral tonight.

[Kung Fu Alex] Done.

Data Entry
Time: 11:26 AM MST
13 April, 2022
Dose: Microdose and Nature Walk

[Electric KT] Logging on…

✦ RE-MEMBER ✦

The Medicine is in you.
The Medicine is in you.
The Medicine is in you.

Wake up.

Data Entry
Time: 8:15 PM MST
17 April, 2022
Dose: Moonlight

[Electric KT] Logging on…

[E.T.] I need healing..

[Electric KT] Is that so?

[E.T.] Yes, I'm not sure what that entails, but you look like the kind of person I'd trust to do it.

[Electric KT] What's got you down?

[E.T.] Worried about the future. Pretty basic.

[Electric KT] Don't sweat it. All we have is now.

[E.T.] I try to stay grounded in that, but it's not always possible.

[Electric KT] What's your sign?

[E.T.] Leo. HBU?

[Electric KT] Aries Sun & Moon. Libra Rising.

[E.T.] Love that. I'm not sure what you're looking for, but if you want to meet up..

[Electric KT] *Thinks to Self. Is this how relationships start on planet Earth? Qualifying sex first.
Age Gap calculation: 17.5 years
Assessment: Legit.
Commit if: E.T. drinks filtered H20, ingests Psilocybin, bonus points for LSD, abstains from alcohol, no psych meds, can French kiss, makes loud noises/dirty talk during sex, funny, open Crown Chakra, lifts weights, vul-

nerable, open Heart Chakra, emotional gauges accessible, calibrated communication system, has car, above average intelligence, Intuitive or ESP dialed in.

[SCANNING] · △⋯→ Soul Star Recognition Detected · △⋯→
[Electric KT] I'm available now, and that's a rarity.

[E.T.] I'm down.

Data Entry
Time: 8:43 PM MST
17 April, 2022
Sun Sign: Leo

[Electric KT] Spits out a bunch of Psychic Healer jargon.

[E.T.] Wow…you're cool.

[Electric KT] *puts on Best of Rock: 70s

⚡✧♎:: [Electric KT] \\::⚡✧ ☥ ✧⚡::// [E.T.] ::♎✧⚡

[Electric KT]

I'll heal you with my

Ω

LOVE

LOVE

LOVE

LOVE

LOVE

LOVE

LOVE

LOVE

[E.T.]

Pronunciation:
/ˈeliet/

✧ ✧ ✧ Uuuuuuuuuuuuuuuuuuuuuhhhhhhhhhhhhhhhhh ✧ ✧ ✧

[MORE]

✧ ✧ ✧ Uuuuuuuuuuuuuuuuuuuuuhhhhhhhhhhhhhhhhh ✧ ✧ ✧

Data Entry
Time: 7:15 PM MST
18 April, 2022
Sun Sign: Leo

[Electric KT] Logging on…

[E.T.] You good?

[Electric KT] Oh come on, you can do better than that.

[E.T.] You're not wrong. I'm being a lazy bum. So tired.

[Electric KT] Bro.

[E.T.] I'm studying. Do you believe in me?

[Electric KT] Of course I do.

[E.T.] :)))

[Electric KT] What are ya thinkin'?

[E.T.] Quite a few things are playing in my mind. Is that just me orrrrr…

[Electric KT] Same.

[E.T.] What parts?

[Electric KT] Well I like kissing you. ❧❧❧❧❧❧❧❧❧❧❧❧❧❧❧❧❧ ❧❧ ✧✧✧ ✧✧✧

[E.T.] Yaaaaaaaaa…I like it too. ♥ ♥ ♥ ♥ ♥ ♥ ♥ ♥ ♥ ♥ ♥ ♥ ♥

[Electric KT] If you want to hang out again..

[E.T.] What would be a good day for tac?

[E.T.] *that

[Electric KT] Wednesday might work.

[E.T.] —————

Data Entry
Time: 6:37 PM MST
20 April, 2022
Dose: Earth Reality

[Electric KT] Logging on…

[Electric KT] Heyy. You still wanna meet up tonight?

[E.T.] Unswipe.

[Electric KT]

IRONSIDE FROM KILL BILL VOL 1 SCREAMS IN BRAIN

Shock Circuit begins.

Stomach punch feeling takes breathe away.

These Humans are fucking dicks.

Why am I even here to help these fuckers.

Nervous System Shock Circuit Fully Engaged.

Gasp of air.

Emotional flooding.

BUT WHY
BUT WHY
BUT WHY
BUT WHY
BUT WHY
BUT WHY
BUT WHY
BUT WHY
BUT WHY
BUT WHY
BUT WHY

I do not understand these assholes.

Data Entry
Time: 7:02 PM MST
20 April, 2022
Dose: Pain

Damn it. Here we go again. This is not worth the sex.

6:38 PM MST {#$*&^!!!!????DRYHEAVECRYINGINSUES>>#$!@&^%*} {#$*&^!!!!????DRYHEAVECRYINGINSUES>>#$!@&^%*} {#$*&^!!!!????DRYHEAVECRYINGINSUES>>#$!@&^%*} {#$*&^!!!!????DRYHEAVECRYINGINSUES>>#$!@&^%*} {#$*&^!!!!????DRYHEAVECRYINGINSUES>>#$!@&^%*} {#$*&^!!!!????DRYHEAVECRYINGINSUES>>#$!@&^%*} {#$*&^!!!!????DRYHEAVECRYINGINSUES>>#$!@&^%*} {#$*&^!!!!????DRYHEAVECRYINGINSUES>>#$!@&^%*} {#$*&^!!!!????DRYHEAVECRYINGINSUES>>#$!@&^%*} {#$*&^!!!!????DRYHEAVECRYINGINSUES>>#$!@&^%*} {#$*&^!!!!????DRYHEAVECRYINGINSUES>>#$!@&^%*} {#$*&^!!!!????DRYHEAVECRYINGINSUES>>#$!@&^%*} {#$*&^!!!!????DRYHEAVECRYINGINSUES>>#$!@&^%*} {#$*&^!!!!????DRYHEAVECRYINGINSUES>>#$!@&^%*} {#$*&^!!!!????DRYHEAVECRYINGINSUES>>#$!@&^%*} {#$*&^!!!!????DRYHEAVE**<<GHOSTING>>**#$!@&^%*} {#$*&^!!!!????DRYHEAVECRYINGINSUES>>#$!@&^%*} {#$*&^!!!!????DRYHEAVECRYINGINSUES>>#$!@&^%*} {#$*&^!!!!????DRYHEAVECRYINGINSUES>>#$!@&^%*} {#$*&^!!!!????DRYHEAVECRYINGINSUES>>#$!@&^%*} {#$*&^!!!!????DRYHEAVECRYINGINSUES>>#$!@&^%*} {#$*&^!!!!????DRYHEAVECRYINGINSUES>>#$!@&^%*} {#$*&^!!!!????DRYHEAVECRYINGINSUES>>#$!@&^%*} {#$*&^!!!!????DRYHEAVECRYINGINSUES>>#$!@&^%*} {#$*&^!!!!????DRYHEAVECRYINGINSUES>>#$!@&^%*} {#$*&^!!!!????DRYHEAVECRYINGINSUES>>#$!@&^%*} {#$*&^!!!!????DRYHEAVECRYINGINSUES>>#$!@&^%*} {#$*&^!!!!????DRYHEAVECRYINGINSUES>>#$!@&^%*} {#$*&^!!!!????DRYHEAVECRYINGINSUES>>#$!@&^%*} {#$*&^!!!!????DRYHEAVECRYINGINSUES>>#$!@&^%*} {#$*&^!!!!????DRYHEAVECRYINGINSUES>>#$!@&^%*} {#$*&^!!!!????DRYHEAVECRYINGINSUES>>#$!@&^%*} {#$*&^!!!!????DRYHEAVECRYINGINSUES>>#$!@&^%*} {#$*&^!!!!????DRYHEAVECRYINGINSUES>>#$!

5 DAYS LATER

These pricks are lucky I'm beyond the murder stage of my evolution.

Data Entry
Time: 7:26 PM MST
21 April, 2022
Dose: Growth

[Electric KT] Logging on…

<ERROR>
/Correction.07:26.01/
[SYSTEM CORRECTION]
{Insert:\\TAG//: here}
shame::shame<shame>shame::shame<shame>shame::shame<shame>
shame::shame<shame> shame::shame<shame>shame::shame<shame>
shame::shame<shame>shame::shame<shame>shame::shame<shame>
shame::shame<shame>shame::shame<shame>shame::shame<shame>
shame::shame<shame> shame::shame<shame>shame::shame<shame>
shame::shame<shame>shame::shame<shame>shame::shame<shame>
shame::shame<shame>shame::shame<shame>shame::shame<shame>
shame::shame<shame> shame::shame<shame>shame::shame<shame>
shame::shame<shame>shame::shame<shame>shame::shame<shame>
shame::shame<shame>shame::shame<shame>shame::shame<shame>
shame::shame<shame> shame::shame<shame>shame::shame<shame>
shame::shame<shame>shame::shame<GHOSTING>::shame<shame>
shame::shame<shame>shame::shame<shame>shame::shame<shame>
shame::shame<shame> shame::shame<shame>shame::shame<shame>
shame::shame<shame>shame::shame<shame>shame::shame<shame>
shame::shame<shame>shame::shame<shame>shame::shame<shame>
shame::shame<shame> shame::shame<shame>shame::shame<shame>
shame::shame<shame>shame::shame<shame>shame::shame<shame>
shame::shame<shame>shame::shame<shame>shame::shame<shame>
shame::shame<shame> shame::shame<shame>shame::shame<shame>
shame::shame<shame>shame::shame<shame>shame::shame<shame>
shame::shame<shame>shame::shame<shame>shame::shame<shame>
shame::shame<shame> shame::shame<shame>shame::shame<shame>
shame::shame<shame>shame::shame<shame>shame::shame<shame>

/Correction.07:27.01/
[RECODING COMPLETE]

Data Entry
Time: 6:37 PM MST
23 April, 2022
Dose: Libido

[Electric KT] Logging on…

God damn it, I'm already horny again.
The [LIBIDO DRIVE] is on overdrive.
Extremely inconvenient when the Humans are serving up shit salad for breakfast.

<:connection low:>

Miss skin contact.
Miss laughter.
Miss kissing.
Miss open hearts.
Miss breaths on my neck.
Miss hands in my hair.
Miss hip bones on my thighs.
Miss squeezes.
Miss gazing eyes.
Miss in-between smiles.
Miss moans and whimpers.
Miss holds and caresses.
Miss whispers in my ear.
Miss your tongue.
Miss you near.
Miss it all.

<:reboot:>

[Electric KT] Logging off.

Data Entry
Time: 3:08 AM MST
24 April, 2022
Dose: Starlight

[Electric KT] Logging on…

[Request] I want to relearn intimacy.

[Universe] Heart expansion lesson initiated.

[Electric KT] Please be gentle. I've had too much pain. I can't take much more.

[Universe] …

W
E
E
P
I
N
G

C
R
I
E
S

T
O

S
L
E
E
P

Data Entry
Time: 10:26AM MST
2 May, 2022
Dose: Buti Yoga

[Electric KT] Logging on…

School of Mastery.
Vibrate High.
Transcend.
Ascend.

◈

Do you speak my language?
I speak in tongues.
They speak in shapes.
Downloads of Light.

◈

I AM the Master,
of my own Energy.
Do you remember?
The amnesia is thick,
Here on Earth.

✳ ✳ ✳ Just breeeeaathe ✳ ✳ ✳

Data Entry
Time: 2:22 AM MST
5 May, 2022
Dose: Meditation

[Electric KT] Logging on…

Move the ENERGY with your mind.
This is just another round of psyops.
My childhood trained me for this.
This contract is almost over.
There is no greater freedom,
Than the freedom of your mind.
No greater victory,
Than regaining it,
after decades of manipulation.
Guantanamo Bay levels of
Intentionally induced confusion.
Hop in deep,
Find your way back out,
Like a god damn Houdini.
In order to expand your mind,
You must first compress it.
So much, that it might implode.
But if you're a Master,
You will break free,
Just before the compression point breaks.
A blueprint deep inside will nudge you,
To seek the Truth serum.
One will wake you up,
And one will put your further to sleep.
Access your Consciousness.
This is a course in Remembering.
Breathe in, breathe out.
Harness your POWER.
Rise above.
Emerge,
With the greatest understanding,
Of all that is Infinite,
Of the Omnipresence.
Of the **I AM**.

Data Entry
Time: 8:49 AM MST
7 May, 2022
Dose: Connection

[Electric KT] Logging on…

[Kung Fu Alex] Send Nudes.

[Electric KT] Send Money.

[Kung Fu Alex] Lol. Find some sucker and survive.

[Electric KT] I was already a prostitute. Marriage. Shittiest invention on Earth. We went over this. Not doing that again, or anything like it.

[Kung Fu Alex] Well shoots. I don't know what to tell ya. I have a garden.

[Electric KT] You're thousands of miles away.

[Kung Fu Alex] Fr. So send me some nudes.

[Electric KT] Gah. Send me a pic of your face for once. Dick pics don't turn me on.

[Kung Fu Alex] They turn me on.

[Electric KT] Brah.

[Kung Fu Alex] Haha. Here's one.

[Electric KT] You're handsome. But you look so serious. You look disturbed.

[Kung Fu Alex] I have ptsd from the future.

[Electric KT] Dude.

[Kung Fu Alex] It's bad. Haven't you seen it? I've been prepping for the last 6 years.

[Electric KT] Don't welcome that reality to set in. That one already played out. I'm trying to bring the other parallel into alignment. The one where the Light has already won.

[Kung Fu Alex] Shoots girl, you're naive.

[Electric KT] Fuck, I really needed that last guy to last longer. What is with this ghosting? Fucking viral bullshit. Earth is whack.

[Kung Fu Alex] Oh you signed up for that assignment? Damn. That's a hardcore shitty one.

[Electric KT] I don't think I signed up for it, but somehow I got reassigned to it. Maybe all that sex I was craving aligned me with it. Apparently I'm perfect for the job.

[Kung Fu Alex] Lol. You are perfect. If I were there, I'd be fucking you right now.

[Electric KT] Stahp.

[Kung Fu Alex] Damn, now you got me horny again.

[Electric KT] I didn't do anything!

[Kung Fu Alex] I know. You're powerful.

[Electric KT] Okay, I'll take that one. Here's a pic. Just for you.

[Kung Fu Alex] Oof. You got me girl.

[Electric KT] I love sex so much. Right when I'm about to hit the [EJECT] button, my Guides are like, "Quick, send her another spicy one nighter to revive her!!"

Then I'm like fine, I'll stick around a little longer.

[Kung Fu Alex] True dat. Same.

[Electric KT] *Sigh..

[Kung Fu Alex] This one really had you seeing stars, huh..

[Electric KT] You know I like I like the sparkly ones.

[Kung Fu Alex] We all do. The reflection.

[Electric KT] I knew E.T. was getting bumped off my field. My signal online started acting all whacky. It was trying to delete him on the dating site without me initiating it.

[Kung Fu Alex] I'm going back to flip phones. My tech doesn't get all bunk like that though. Dunno what's up with that. The robots show up in person for me. That's why I gotta stay in hiding. Yano.

[Electric KT] It's a psychic thing. Signal gets all jazzed up when something's about to go down or I'm tuned super high. It's annoying.

You gotta learn that invisibility cloak, bro. So you don't have to physically hide.
Sheesh Jedi. That's some amateur shit.

[Kung Fu Alex] I'm gonna make my dick go invisible, right inside your…

[Electric KT] How do I get stationed with you guys..

[Kung Fu Alex] You chose me. We are all each other's subconscious. You know this.

[Electric KT] *Eye roll. Anyways, I knew he was about to hit the mini [eject] button on me. I could feel it a week prior, coming in strong. Had me all buzzing in the bad way.

[Kung Fu Alex] Go chase that deep dick girl.

[Electric KT] Can't. Don't chase. But I dropped him my cell and real name, so he can stalk me later. Ha.

[Kung Fu Alex] Nice.

[Electric KT] I'm all about those 4-hour sensual and passionate sessions with a bunch of life chit chat in between. That's how I like to get down. Here on Earth.

[Kung Fu Alex] That's what's up.

[Electric KT] Intensity.

[Kung Fu Alex] She likes it lit. Electric Kay-tee.

Alright girl. You'll be aight. Gn 4 now.

[Electric KT] Sweet dreams.

Data Entry
Time: 12:15 PM MST
10 May, 2022
Dose: Microdose

[Electric KT] Logging on…

With childlike curiosity,
The innocence of love,
Alchemize this creation,
Connected from above.

Every time you drop to a lower frequency,
it has the (PE) potential energy to (KE) catapult you into a higher level
than the last.
Ebb and Flow.
Surrender.
Let go.
Rise Up.
Vibrate High.

Enlightenment	700–1000	Omega	
Peace	600		
Joy	540	Ultimate Consciousness	
Love	500		Expanded
Reason	400	Pure Tao	
Acceptance	350		
Willingness	310	Flow	
Neutrality	250		
Courage	200		
Pride	175	Getting By	
Anger	150		Contacted
Desire	125		
Fear	100	Suffering	
Grief	75		
Apathy	50		
Guilt	30	Alpha	
Shame	20		

❥ ❥ ❥ (((Speak to me in Hertz))) ❥ ❥ ❥

Data Entry
Time: 8:14 PM MST
12 May, 2022
Dose: Of Caution

[Electric KT] Logging on…

[Space Troi] Wanna see you.

[Electric KT] That's what they all say.

[Space Troi] No. I'm not all them.

[Electric KT] They say that too!

[Space Troi] Welp.

[Electric KT] Lol. And then they ghost. I know the drill.

[Space Troi] You're bringing me down by saying that.

[Electric KT] What do you really want?

[Space Troi] To meet.

[Electric KT] And then what?

[Space Troi] Not sure. I don't really like to think that far ahead.

[Electric KT] Okk. I just need a friend right now.

[Space Troi] I'm totally fine with that. I'm really easy and not judgmental. It would be cool to meet and become friends.

[Electric KT] Good. I need that.

Data Entry
Time: 7:27 AM MST
13 May, 2022
Sun Sign: Taurus

[Electric KT] Logging on…

✧

✧

Surf Lover

✧ 干 ✧ Troi ✧ 干 ✧

Starseed Whisperer

Panty Soaker

Landlocked Dreamer

Sparkly Heart

Trojan Walls

Translation:

"foot soldier"

Origin: Ancient Greece

✧ 干 ✧ [Electric KT] Take me through the sparkly waves with you. [Troi] ✧ 干 ✧

✧ 干 ✧ [Troi] I wanna feel the current until we wash up on shore. [Electric KT] ✧ 干 ✧

✧ 干 ✧ [Troi] ○ ∘ • ✧ ○ ∘ • ✧ Rn ✧ • ∘ ○ ✧ • ∘ [Electric KT] ✧ 干 ✧

Data Entry
Time: 10:10 AM MST
14 May, 2022
Dose: Double Microdose

[Electric KT] Logging on…

[Hue–Mans]

350 Hz ——————————————————————— 440 Hz

[Electric KT] Dang, they're completely offline today.

Data Entry
Time: 11:33 PM MST
15 May, 2022
Dose: 1 hit of Love

[Electric KT] Logging on…

[Space Troi] Come see me.

[Electric KT] I'm sleeping.

[Space Troi] Lame.

[Electric KT] Please don't call me lame.

[Space Troi] Ok. I'll stop. I'm sorry.

[Electric KT] I need rest.

[Space Troi] Wish I was cuddling you rn.

[Electric KT] Me too. Some comfort.

[Space Troi] I feel that.

[Electric KT] I wanna feel you next to me.

[Space Troi] Me too. I love skin on skin contact.

[Electric KT] It's the best. I want to feel yours.

[Space Troi] You will. Good night b.

Data Entry
Time: 4:01 AM MST
16 May, 2022
Dose: Meditation

[Electric KT] Logging on…

[DATA LOG] The trauma programs here are viral. They have always been viral, but AI is having a hay day with technology and the ability to spread trauma quickly and widely. The access to low frequencies is wide open with technology and social media. Despite it being intangible, is it effectively more damaging the the Human System. The disconnection synthesizes the trauma for Humans. They are severely compromised.

[TRAUMA LOG]

<//physical abuse//>
<//mental abuse//>
<//emotional abuse//>
<//financial abuse//>
<//sexual abuse//>
<//bullying//>
<//spanking//>
<//dunce hats//>
<//molestation//>
<//mocking//>
<//sarcasm//>
<//rape//>
<//doxing//>
<//slut shaming//>
<//dick shaming//>
<//cyber bullying//>
<//revenge porn//>
<//ghosting//>

Data Entry
Time: 4:23 PM MST
17 May, 2022
Dose: Daydreaming

[Electric KT] Logging on…

[Electric KT] This is me last time I was on the beach in 2020.

[Space Troi] No way. I love the beach. Which one?

[Electric KT] Miami.

[Space Troi] U prob look so amazing in a bikini. wow.

[Electric KT] U wanna see?

[Space Troi] !!!

[Electric KT] You first.

[Space Troi] Show me babe.

[Electric KT] I was a lifeguard, so I'm used to being in my swimsuit all day.

[Space Troi] I did that too!! Ahhaha.

[Electric KT] Let me see.

[Space Troi] I don't have any. I just have like bare nudes. hahahaha.

[Electric KT] Send nudes.

[Space Troi] What? You want my nudes?

[Electric KT] Kidding!!

[Space Troi] Are you. I probably would have sent them;)

[Electric KT] Lol.

[Space Troi] Can I trust you?

[Electric KT] Yes.

[Space Troi] You promise?

[Electric KT] I promise.

[Space Troi] ○ ∘ • ✧ ○ ∘ • ✧ ○ ∘ • ✧ dreamy ✧ • ∘ ○ ✧ • ∘ ○ ✧ • ∘ ○

[Electric KT] Troi!!

[Space Troi] What!!

[Electric KT] You're sexy:)

[Space Troi] Now you. Ru shy?

[Electric KT] A little. I'm comfortable with my body, but cautious with my feelings.

[Space Troi] I feel that. I feel comfortable with you.

[Electric KT] Same.

[Space Troi] Good. Do u hv any pics that are teasing?

[Electric KT] Maybe..

[Space Troi] Can I see?

[Electric KT] Okay but can I trust YOU?

[Space Troi] Yes I promise.

[Electric KT] ✧ ○ ∘ • ✧ ○ ∘ • ✧ ○ ∘ • melting • ∘ ○ ✧ • ∘ ○ ✧ • ∘ ○ ✧

[Space Troi] Holy fuck. Ugh. KT, you're so sexy.

[Electric KT] ⋆ Swells

       ✧ 干 ✧ [Electric KT] Love me. [Troi] ✧ 干 ✧

       ✧ 干 ✧ [Troi] I already do. [Electric KT] ✧ 干 ✧

Data Entry
Time: 5:05 PM MST
18 May, 2022
Dose: Double Microdose

[Electric KT] Logging on…

Data Log: You can't talk about the robots to the robots.

Collective Reading: Zero D

5 mins later…

Collective Reading: Fuck, now it's -5D

??//:<BlockAiConsciousnessSPAMprograms>:\\??

Data Entry
Time: 1:58 PM MST
19 May, 2022
Dose: Saltwater Waves

[Electric KT] Logging on…

[Space Troi] Hey.

[Electric KT] Hey what.

[Space Troi] Miss ya.

[Electric KT] Miss you too.

[Space Troi] When are we gonna hang?

[Electric KT] Make it happen.

[Space Troi] I'm working 12s. I know I suck.

[Electric KT] I can drive to you? We can sleep. Lol:)

[Space Troi] I'm switching to days soon. I can't wait. Night shift sucks so bad.

[Electric KT] I feel ya. Winter is hard.

[Space Troi] Winter sucks. I hate the sun going down so early.

[Electric KT] Same.

[Space Troi] I miss the ocean. Feeling the water and the waves. The sky. Ugh so good it's like a high. Have you surfed before?

[Electric KT] No, but I went backpacking in Hawaii. I almost didn't come back. It was so gorgeous. I was so happy. I woke up with the sun, and fell asleep with the waves:) That's the way it should be.

[Space Troi] I agree. I could totally see you being a Hawaii girl.

[Electric KT] I would love to live near the beach. The mountains and beach. My favorite places:)

[Space Troi] Same. I used to park my van by the beach and keep the doors open or windows down at night. It was so nice to listen to the waves crash. Ahhh.

[Electric KT] Sounds beautiful. I wanna go.

[Space Troi] It was. Me too. Ur so cool KT.

[Electric KT] You're so sweet. *zzzz ☾

[Space Troi] * zzzz ☾

Data Entry
Time: 4:21 AM MST
20 May, 2022
Dose: Microdose

[Electric KT] Logging on…

Stars shapes don't fit into square holes.

It doesn't take a genius to learn a shape sorter.

These idiots are failing at toddler circle time exercises.

<:remove::judgement:>

They don't need a brain break. They need a brain "on."

<:remove::judgement:>

They don't need to go back to grad school. They need to go back to Pre-school…unless they've ruined that one too.

<:remove::cynicism:>

Stop dimming our LIGHT!

<:remove::anger:>

Let's draw shapes together.

<adding::love:>

Now let's color them.

<adding::more::love>

Let's make the shapes dance and sing.

<infinite::love>

My shape loves your shape.

<::unity::>

Data Entry
Time: 9:18 PM MST
20 May, 2022
Dose: Magic

[Electric KT] Logging on…

[Space Troi] Come back:(

[Electric KT] Why..

[Space Troi] I like talking to ya.

[Electric KT] I like you too.

[Space Troi] Aw. I like when you send selfies. I like your cute face.

[Electric KT] Okay, but you too.

[Space Troi] Of course.

[Electric KT] ♥ ✧ ♥ ✧ ♥ ✧ ♥ ✧ ♥ ✧ ♥ ✧ ♥ ✧ ♥ ✧ ♥ ✧ ♥ ✧

[Space Troi] *hearts image

I wanna go on an adventure with you.

[Electric KT] With me?

[Space Troi] Yea you.

[Electric KT] Me too. Let me see you now.

[Space Troi] ♉♥ ✧ ♉♥ ✧ ♉♥ ✧ ♉♥ ✧ ♉♥ ✧ ♉♥ ✧ ♉♥ ✧

[Electric KT] *hearts image

Aren't we on one?

Data Entry
Time: 7:06 AM MST
21 May, 2022
Dose: Turquoise

[Electric KT] Logging on…

[Space Troi] What ru doin bb?

[Electric KT] Watching the sun come up. You?

[Space Troi] About to go to sleep.

[Electric KT] Yeah? Here's a song. I've been listening to it all weekend. It puts me in the best mood.

*Sends link:

✧ ✳ ✧ ✳ ✧ ✳ ✧ ✳ |Crystal Blue Persuasion|✧ ✳ ✧ ✳ ✧ ✳ ✧ ✳ ✧

[Space Troi] I LOVE MUSIC LIKE THIS

[Electric KT] It's so dreamy.

[Space Troi] I might need a ride to the airport next week. How do you feel about me staying the night?

[Electric KT] I can do that. You're more than welcome to come crash on my couch;) I'd like us to meet.

[Space Troi] Your couch!!!!!

[Electric KT] Hahaha kidding!!!!

[Space Troi] Lame.

[Electric KT] Don't! You know I want to sleep on your chest:)

[Space Troi] Oh really? I'd like that.

[Electric KT] Let's do it.

[Space Troi] It's okay. The airport is too far. I'd have to leave at 4 am.

[Electric KT] You could Uber from my place.

[Space Troi] Nah, it's too much to ask. I'll figure it out.

[Electric KT] It's up to you.

[Space Troi] We can hang when I get back.

[Electric KT] Ok, safe travels:)

[Space Troi] Thanks.

Data Entry
Time: 7:32 AM MST
26 May, 2022
Dose: Yoga Flow

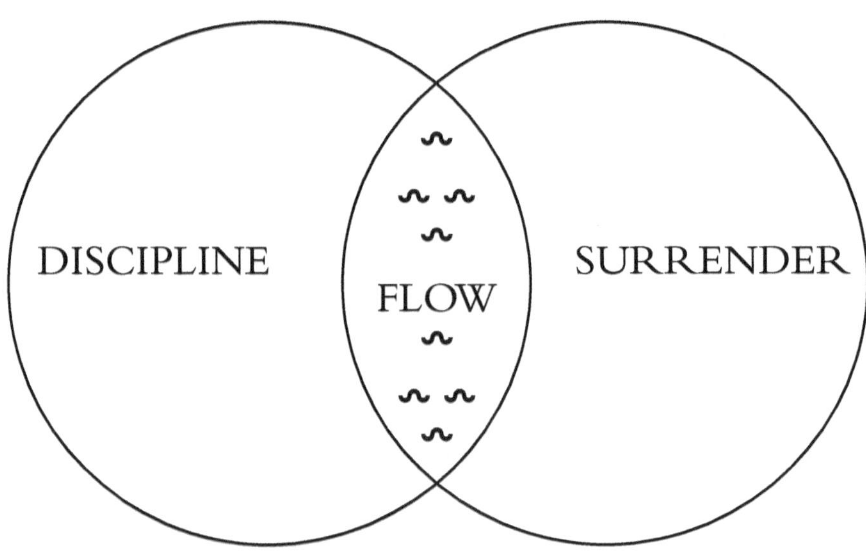

Data Entry
Time: 8:50 PM MST
27 May, 2022
Dose: Lust

[Electric KT] Logging on…

[Space Troi] Whacha doin?

[Electric KT] Laying in bed.

[Space Troi] Wish I was there with you rn.

[Electric KT] Me too.

[Space Troi] What kind of sexual things do you like?

[Electric KT] What? Lol. Omg. I love French kissing. It's my favorite. Do you like it?

[Space Troi] Of course. I bet you're a great kisser. I bet you're amazing at everything.

[Electric KT] I bet you are too.

[Space Troi] I am. And I'm a good licker.

[Electric KT] Troi!!

[Space Troi] What! I wanna lick you.

[Electric KT] Mm:)

[Space Troi] I want to do everything with you.

Data Entry
Time: 6:10 AM MST
28 May, 2022
Dose: Sun Salutation

[Electric KT] Logging on…

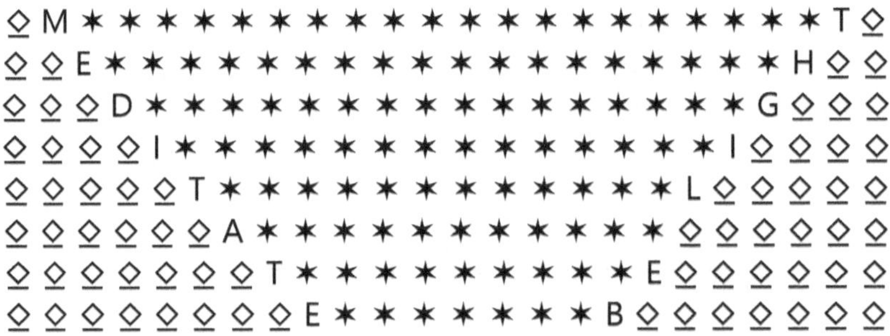

Until you reach stillness.
Then embrace darkness.
Return to Light.

Data Entry
Time: 3:33 PM MST
29 May, 2022
Dose: Third Eye Clarity

[Electric KT] Logging on…

[Electric KT] Do you meditate?

[Space Troi] Not much. I wish I did more.

[Electric KT] It's good. Helps make everything crystal clear. ◊ ◊ ◊ ◊ ◊

Mellow. ◊ ◊ ◊ ◊ ◊

Aligned. ◊ ◊ ◊ ◊ ◊

[Space Troi] That sounds nice.

[Electric KT] Do you get into all the Consciousness concepts surrounding meditation? Like manifesting, collective consciousness, etc.

[Space Troi] Not too sure. Surfing was meditative.

[Electric KT] *Fuck. He can't remember yet. I wonder if he microdoses. He's got to want to wake up. Why else is he talking to me..

[Space Troi] Are you in bed?

[Electric KT] Not yet.

[Space Troi] I'm naked;)

[Electric KT] *Sigh. I want him to be awake. I don't want to talk to the [ego] anymore. I want to talk to his soul. The spirit that keeps touching my heart and making me feel warm and loved. The one that lights up like the sun, and purrs like the ocean, next to my heart.

[Electric KT] Manifesting is a concept that everything is energy, like on a level of quantum mechanics. Your observation of something, even a thought, makes it come into being—into form. When you feel the emotion of it, like you've already won an award or something, that makes it even stronger and come into fruition faster.

[Space Troi] Ahhh, I see.

[Electric KT] *But does he see?

⸱⸱⸱→ ☾ Not with his third eye. ☾ ←⸱⸱⸱

But I want him to. It's so lonely without it.

[Space Troi] I wanna see you rn. I can't help it. I'm into you b.

[Electric KT] Collective consciousness is the concept that if you think it, then it already exists on some parallel plane. And you just have to align, to bring it into your reality. It's like an idea is out there in the ethers, and you can snag it. Hence why a person on one side of the world may have the same idea as another on the opposite side, without ever having met. That kind of thing. Another example would be when musicians or artists feel like the music just "downloads" to them from somewhere. As if it already exists and they channeled it.

[Space Troi] *crickets

[Electric KT] *Fuuuuuuck. He's not awake. That [ego] is stepping in hardcore with the "b" talk. It's fun when it's play-ful, but not when it's play-er. Player player two, get out of my hard drive. I can feel his box brain straining.
His wires are locked up with no flow.
He needs flow.
He needs some saltwater, ASAP.
Someone bring him the OCEAN 〜 〜 〜 〜 〜 〜 〜 〜 〜 〜 〜 〜

[Troi] ⧌ 千 Subconscious Self ESP 千 ⧌ I can hear you. I just like to say b. Cuz you're my baby, and I want to protect you. You're so beautiful, and sometimes I can't believe you're talking to me.

[Electric KT] ⚠ 千 Subconscious Self ESP 千 Of course I am. I adore you. You're so handsome and kind. But I want you to hear me out there. I need you out there. I can feel your warm, protective spirit. That's why I can't let go.

[Troi] ⚠ 千 Subconscious Self ESP 千 That's what I came here for. To serve and protect, especially women. But they always get so mad at me. Why? I can't do it. But I want to. I don't know how.

[Electric KT] ⚠ 千 Subconscious Self ESP 千 You're already doing it. You're just not aware, so you get side-tracked. We all get confused down here. It's the amnesia, and all their systems are whack. As Starseeds, we have so much love in our hearts, and we don't know how to direct it. Our Light. Everyone is drawn to it, and then everyone pushes it away. It hurts.

[Troi] ⚠ 千 Subconscious Self ESP 千 Yes. Exactly! It hurts so bad. I can't stand it. I want to hold you. I want the other things too, to kiss you from head to toe, and rub your body all over. That's what I would do if I woke up next to you every day.

[Electric KT] ⚠ 千 Subconscious Self ESP 千 I would love that so much. It sounds like heaven.

[Troi] ⚠ 千 Subconscious Self ESP 千 I would hold you. No one could touch you in the ways you don't like. No one could hurt you. I wouldn't let them. You're so beautiful. I'd keep you safe.

[Electric KT] ⚠ 千 Subconscious Self ESP 千 You make my heart melt. I want to be safe in your arms, and rest my head on your chest so badly. Meet me out there. Please.

[Troi] ⚠ 千 Subconscious Self ESP 千 I'm trying. I really am. But I don't know how to manage all this time. I do what I need, and then I run out. I can't find the time. Wtf is with this time?

[Electric KT] ⚠ 千 Subconscious Self ESP 千 Time is complete fuckery down there.

[Troi] ⚠ 干 Subconscious Self ESP 干 Right now, in the present moment, I can't make it work. I haven't figured it out.

[Electric KT] ⚠ 干 Subconscious Self ESP 干 That's because you are not in the Present Moment. You are in the matrix.

[Troi] ⚠ 干 Subconscious Self ESP 干 Oh shit. Then where are we now?

[Electric KT] ⚠ 干 Subconscious Self ESP 干 The in-between.

[Troi] ⚠ 干 Subconscious Self ESP 干 Do I have to go back?

[Electric KT] ⚠ 干 Subconscious Self ESP 干 Yes, until you wake up. I will miss you. Come see me in the astral, space cowboy.

[Troi] ⚠ 干 Subconscious Self ESP 干 I will. Where there's no time, I can weave time:)

[Electric KT] ⚠ 干 Subconscious Self ESP 干 I know, you're magical:)

✧ 干 ✧

✧

✧

✧ 干 ✧ [Electric KT] Meet me here. [Troi] ✧ 干 ✧

✧ 干 ✧ [Troi] I will. [Electric KT] ✧ 干 ✧

✧ 干 ✧

✧

✧ 干 ✧ [Electric KT] Will you re-member? [Troi] ✧ 干 ✧

✧ 干 ✧ [Troi] Yes. Cross my heart. [Electric KT] ✧ 干 ✧

✧ 干 ✧ [Electric KT] Okay. I trust you. [Troi] ✧ 干 ✧

✧ 干 ✧ [Troi] I trust you too. [Electric KT] ✧ 干 ✧

✧ 干 ✧

✧

✧ 干 ✧ [Electric KT] I luv you. In my heart. I feel it. [Troi] ✧ 干 ✧

✧ 干 ✧ [Troi] I do too b. It's throbbing. [Electric KT] ✧ 干 ✧

✧ 干 ✧ [Electric KT] Mine is too. It feels so good, it almost hurts. [Troi]
✧ 干 ✧

✧ 干 ✧ [Troi] I know. Same. [Electric KT] ✧ 干 ✧

✧ 干 ✧

✧ 干 ✧

✧

✧

[Space Troi] How wet is your pussy?

[Electric KT] Very.

[Space Troi] Show me.

[Electric KT] No way!! I never show pics like that!

[Space Troi] Video?

[Electric KT] Maybe..

[Space Troi] Ugh. I wanna see. Turn the flash on this time.

[Electric KT] Omg you wanna see everything don't you.

[Space Troi] Yes. I can't wait to see your lips around my cock.

[Electric KT] Do you want to watch me?

[Space Troi] Omg yes. I bet you stare up with those sexy eyes.

[Electric KT] This is what I'm gonna do to your dick when I see you.

*sends video ○ ∘ • ✧ ○ ∘ • ✧ ○ ∘ • ✧ ○ ∘ • ❥ ❥ ❥ • ∘ ○ ✧ • ∘ ○ ✧ • ∘ ○ ✧ • ∘ ○

[Space Troi] Fuck, KT. You're so hot. I want you so fucking bad. You make me so hard.

[Electric KT] I love how hard you get.

[Space Troi] You're so dirty too. I love it.

*sends video ○ ∘ • ✧ ○ ∘ • ✧ ○ ∘ • ✧ ○ ∘ • ❥ ❥ ❥ • ∘ ○ ✧ • ∘ ○ ✧ • ∘ ○ ✧ • ∘ ○

[Electric KT] Mm. Troi. Fuck. I want to feel you inside me.

[Space Troi] I bet you feel amazing. I wanna make you moan.

[Electric KT] I love being loud.

[Space Troi] I love that. I'm gonna make you scream.

[Electric KT] You make me so hot. I'm so turned on. I'm having a hard time stopping.

[Space Troi] Me too. I'm gonna fuck you so many different ways. I'm gonna make your thighs tremble. I can't wait.

[Electric KT] I want to rub you all over me and leave you there all day.

[Space Troi] Make me cum baby. Rn.

[Electric KT] *sends video ○ ∘ • ✧ ○ ∘ • ✧ ○ ∘ • ✧ ○ ∘ • ❤ ❤ ❤ • ∘ ○ ✧ • ∘ ○ ✧ • ∘ ○ ✧ • ∘ ○

[Space Troi] *sends pic ○ ∘ • ✧ ○ ∘ • ✧ ○ ∘ • ✧ ○ ∘ • ❤ ❤ ❤ • ∘ ○ ✧ • ∘ ○ ✧ • ∘ ○ ✧ • ∘ ○

[Electric KT] *hearts image

[Space Troi] I gotta sleep. I gotta work so early. I'm tired.

[Electric KT] I know. I'll be thinking of you. Good nite.

[Space Troi] Good nite.

Data Entry
Time: 6:43 PM MST
1 June, 2022
Dose: Infinity

[Electric KT] Logging on…

[✧ • △ • \\ ○ // • △ • ✧ New Formula ✧ • △ \\ • ○ // • △ • ✧]

2GIVE + 2RECIEVE → 2LOVE

[⊨New Equation⊨]

1 + 1 =

✧ ∫ Infinity ∫ ✧

Data Entry
Time: 1:11 AM MST
2 June, 2022
Dose: Astral Love

✧ 千 ✧

✧ 千 ✧

✧

✧

✧ [Troi] Holds face. Caresses shoulder. Kisses neck. [Electric KT] ✧

✧ [Electric KT] Runs fingers over hair. Down chest. Kisses lips. [Troi] ✧

Breathes relief

✧ 千 ✧

✧

❤ ❤ ❤ ❤ ❤ ❤ [Electric KT] ⟶ ❤ ❤ ⟵ [Troi] ❤ ❤ ❤ ❤ ❤ ❤

✧ 千 ✧

[Electric KT] I wish it could last forever. [Troi]

[Troi] I know. In here it does. [Electric KT]

✧ 千 ✧

[Electric KT] Hold me. [Troi]

[Troi] Forever KT. Forever. [Electric KT]

✧ 千 ✧

✧ 千 ✧

✧

✧

Data Entry
Time: 8:08 AM MST
3 June, 2022
Dose: O2

[Electric KT] Logging on…

[Research]

US84750834934758345864385698347598347598375873459739874862
87556480040258736B2
Status: *patent pending*

Description:

Abstract

Geometric systems and energetic methods are expressed to dynamically apply a design across a holographic display field composed of visual surfaces to create an impression of a single, unified aesthetic. Geometries, physics, and layers of consciousness are used to formulate the display within the field. A source image can be mapped, using the original blueprint, to generate one or more field maps. An individual expression can be generated from the field maps, according to various factors, including the individual emotional package layouts and layers. Some embodiments allow the generated expression to be previewed, the entire display field to be virtually previewed, and/or the expression to be output. The output unified expression is high frequency, zero point oriented, expanded sacral energetic layer, with an ability to transmute and leap into parallel quantum fields.

[Electric KT] Fuck. They are trying to patent my soul.

Data Entry
Time: 8:09 AM MST
3 June, 2022
Dose: Panic

[Electric KT] Logging on…

<:///◉!!!MAYDAY!!!◉\\\:>

<:///◉!!!MAYDAY!!!◉\\\:>

<:///◉!!!MAYDAY!!!◉\\\:>

<:///◉!!!MAYDAY!!!◉\\\:>

<:///◉!!!MAYDAY!!!◉\\\:>

[LIGHT COUNCIL] We see it. Emergency ejection initiated.

[Electric KT] Thank you.

I might miss it here.

*the sex

*the plants

*the ocean

*the mountains

*the music

*the beauty

*his eyes

*her eyes

*all. that. love.

Data Entry
Time: 5:55 PM MST
5 June, 2022
Dose: Time Travel

[Electric KT] Merkabah engaged.

[LIGHT COUNCIL] Portal Open. Brace for travel.

Earth

is

Whack.

[Electric KT] Beaming out. Return to Light.

About the Author:

Katie is a mother, artist, writer, psychic, energy healer, teacher, creator, and otherwise unsuspecting inhabitant of Earth. She enjoys sharing her journey beyond the falsehood of normalcy and into the flow of consciousness. Her intention is to serve as a clear vessel of Light and inspire seekers of the beyond to embrace their quest with an open heart. She holds multiple certificates in clairvoyance and has post-graduate studies in mindfulness-based transpersonal counseling. Katie is an advocate of plant medicine and the gates of consciousness they have the potential to open. When she is not navigating the matrix, she is immersed in discovering the beauty of Earth with her daughters and cuddling their Norwegian Forest cat, Alpine. She enjoys rock climbing, CrossFit, yoga, music of many genres, sunrises, sunsets, fresh water, wildflowers, clear night skies, laughter, deep eye gazing, the orchestra of nature, and losing sense of time.

www.ingramcontent.com/pod-product-compliance
Lightning Source LLC
Chambersburg PA
CBHW020117310726
48970CB00002B/680